Ron Louthan has knocked the proverbial ball out of the park with his latest children's/moral compass outing. I love this book! A good read for adults and children alike.
A rollicking fun adventure with three of the most charming characters you'll ever meet (whether in person or on the page). This book is a winner! Do yourself a favor, read it to your younger pals if you think reading kid lit isn't your cup of tea and take the ride with Hoggy, Froggy and Ernie.

Skip Schoolnik

Producer/Director

Fast paced, lots of mystery, great characters and great locations. Ron Louthan has written a fascinating tale of some very "unlikely" characters on a great adventure in a bazaar world that has plenty of action and intrigue. I would recommend this to anyone.

Michael Tennesen
Author, The Next Species, Simon and Schuster
Duke University Media Fellow

Hop on board and join the escapade as an earthbound woodpecker, a celebrated broad-jumping frog and a dancing pig steer their Harley through the highways of California in search of enlightenment. Rich in imagination and humor, Mr. Louthan brings to life a vivid tale for young and old to embrace, whether reading aloud, acting out scenes or enjoying alone. It's a read you and your school age children won't want to miss.

Marcia Nicholson
Mother of two; Masters in Special Education

Ron Louthan's book, ***The Unlikely Confederacy of Hoggy, Froggy and Ernie*** tells of a fantastical journey by three improbable friends - a pig, a frog and a woodpecker- along the coast of California. The story is filled with adventure, malevolence, pathos, and friendships, along with a dash of mystical spiritualism, while still imparting historical, cultural and geographical awareness.

Louthan skillfully brings life to all of the characters as well as the enchanting locations. The language is realistic and the "surfer-speak" imbedded into the story adds a fun element. The Unlikely Confederacy of Hoggy, Froggy and Ernie is a complete delight and readers of all ages will enjoy the eccentric characters, magical secrets and witty plot.

Dr. Candace Poindexter
Director of Child and Adolescent Literacy
Loyola Marymount University
Los Angeles, California

The story is always moving and the characters rarely stop on their travels. ...different and funny, a great book and really fun.

Arthur Treloar Age 14, Year 8
St Leo's Catholic College
Sydney, New South Wales
Australia

Mr. Louthan has crafted a very clever story. Part travelogue, part adventure, it is a classic quest fable with a side order of humor and political satire. Although targeted for young readers, it has a little something for everyone – ages 5 to 85. Categorizing this story is risky business and you do so at your own peril as it is unique in its structure.

He takes an unlikely premise (a pig, a frog and a woodpecker traveling together on a three wheeled Harley) and makes it completely believable. Combining Vedic myth with contemporary culture and technology, he creates a story that reels you in from the first page. This really is an Unlikely Confederacy.

Bishop Daniel J. Dahl DD
Honolulu, Hawaii

The Unlikely Confederacy of Hoggy, Froggy and Ernie by Ron Louthan is a rollicking adventure-quest story with a wittily conceived plot melding a Wizard of Oz theme and a Tolkien-esque dark backdrop with a zany Tom Robbins sensibility.
Louthan manages to convey a spiritual message in a funny, ironic and suspenseful way following the journey of a pig, a frog and a woodpecker on their path to enlightenment (learning to fly). As in the Wizard of OZ their road is menaced by evil forces but with the powers of some shape-shifting allies they reach their destination.
The main characters are well developed and the setting, Swami's Beach and Big Sur in California, is beautifully described. This story can be read at many levels and is suitable for all ages.

John Galbraith
Teacher, English Literature
Venice High School, Venice Beach, California

Una *"Confederacion Unica"* que te atrapa, te entretiene, y te hace reir y enamorarte de sus personajes, con una cuota sutil de sabiduria y ternura.
Quiero mas!

Ximena Carey
Mother of three; Santiago, Chile

The Unlikely Confederacy of Hoggy, Froggy and Ernie is a page-turner that kicks readers out of their ordinary life, into adventures of many possibilities, free, rich and vibrant. There's understated music in author Ron Louthan's text. The experience is multilayer – not only verbal, but also emotional and mythical. The author possesses an enormous background in research which he weaves into events and characters, but makes it just easy enough to unravel the mysteries without working up a sweat.

Rodney Charles
Author of the bestselling *Every Day a Miracle Happens*

A delightful and entertaining story winding up the California coast and into the magical and wondrous redwoods, a natural wonder of the world. Richly depicts the power of gentle, kind creatures that have lived, like the trees, for thousands of years. It has the wisdom and fun of hobbit-like creatures. The author, apparently, has done some mental journeys himself to be able to create such an exciting morality play.

Jon Artz; Attorney at Law,
Los Angeles, California

The Unlikely Confederacy of Hoggy, Froggy and Ernie, grabbed me and my imagination from the first paragraph. Like a fable it is packed with layers of deeper meaning beyond the zany adventure of three friends on a road trip. And like a great novel it left me hungry for more....."hungry as a woodpecker with a headache"! Read it today and get ready to really enjoy the ride.

Torrie Flink
Former CEO, Zacharias Center
President, Social Action Advisors Lld.
Chicago, Illinois

After reading this book there is one thing for certain. I will never eat *Pork, Frogs Legs, or Woodpecker Wings* again.

Dayton Turner, Artisan
Los Angeles, California

I think that ***"The Unlikely Confederacy of Hoggy, Froggy and Ernie"*** is a great book. I love the creative characters and interesting storyline. I like how the main characters are all animals.
My favourite part is when the Rakshasas fought the good guys.

Tom Treloar Age 11, Year 7
St. Leo's Catholic College
Sydney, New South Wales
Australia

Reminiscent of *"Alice In Wonderland"*... visually descriptive and lucid. There are basic lessons to be learned from the strengths and vulnerabilities of the characters and they are aptly pointed out by a combination of everyday language and metaphysical descriptions of spiritual history.
This is a marvelous tale that should be made into an animated film.

Craig Simmons
Commercial Pilot, Actor, Screenwriter, Musician
Aspen, Colorado

I was hooked within the first page. Ron Louthan has done a superb job writing ***The Unlikely Confederacy Of Hoggy, Froggy , and Ernie.*** He mixed mystical with reality, the impossible with the possible and the new with the old. The book has the normal story line that most books have but with a twist.

Rebecca Basclain, Age 11.
Sydney, New South Wales
Australia

"...subtle and timeless lessons about friendship, loyalty and trust."

Jim O'Connor, Retired Teacher
North Eugene High School
Eugene, Oregon

Few writers are able to capture such a diverse audience. Mr. Louthan's colorful depiction of a band of unique cohorts embarking on a sublimely unique journey plumbs the depths of danger and magical moments of awareness as they arrive at a universal truth... anything is possible!

MJ Mazzitelli, Wine Enthusiast

Mr. Louthan's *The Unlikely Confederacy Of Hoggy, Froggy and Ernie* is a well crafted and intriguing tale of three loveable and unique characters as they set off on an adventurous journey through well know California locales. It's like comfort food for the imagination. Unlikely Confederacy completely captivates the reader from one chapter to the next and when the story reaches its unforgettable climax the only thing that is missing is the sequel!

Melinda Browne
Actor, Voice Performance Coach
Los Angeles, California

THE UNLIKELY CONFEDERACY

OF

HOGGY, FROGGY AND ERNIE

Ron Louthan

The Unlikely Confederacy
of Hoggy, Froggy and Ernie

Ron Louthan

Published by 1st World Publishing
P.O. Box 2211, Fairfield, Iowa 52556
tel: 641-209-5000 • fax: 866-440-5234
web: www.1stworldpublishing.com

First Edition

LCCN: 2012955974
SoftCover ISBN: 978-1-4218-8655-8
HardCover ISBN: 978-1-4218-8656-5
eBook ISBN: 978-1-4218-8657-2

Cover and Interior Illustrations: Mikaila Maidment

ACKNOWLEDGEMENTS

Kudos and karmic kickbacks to the following people, without whose help this story would still be in the incubator.

Rodney Charles for babysitting me through the literary potholes and minefields, providing a smooth trip down the publishing highway.

Marilyn Muerth, Word Processing Wizardess and Editor Extraordinaire.

Chilean Cosmic Earth Mama Ximena Carey and Frequent Flyer Fox Vidya Schechtman for the use of their beautiful names.

Dawn Rachel Hutchins whose world class garden and amazing rescue animals provided inspiration.

And Aussie-girl Sue Warner whose confidence never wavered, even when mine did.

Ron Louthan

Topanga Canyon, California
November, 2012

AUTHORS NOTE

Many authors go to great lengths to proclaim the fictitious nature of their work.

The characters and places, they say, are merely products of their imagination and should be taken as such. That is not the case here. All the players and locals in this story are real and the events described herein are accurate to the extent that memory will allow.

Ron Louthan

Catalina Island, California
December, 2012

PART ONE
SWAMI'S BEACH

CHAPTER 1

Ernie was in the zone.

Or so he thought. He was in the tube, crouched low on his board, surrounded by water and shootin' the curl. A surfer's dream, the perfect wave. Perfect, that is, until it crested over his head, curled under his board and sucked him deep into the churning water below. Over and over he tumbled like a sock in a washing machine until it finally spit him out, planting him beak first in the sand like some upside down feathered scarecrow. Beak first? Feathered? Yes. You see, Ernie is a woodpecker.

Froggy watched all this with amusement. It wasn't the first time he had seen his friend wipe out in a tumbler. He paddled to shore and when he got to Ernie, grabbed him by the wings and pulled him from the shallow water with a sucking sound. Ernie came up spitting sand.

"You okay?" said Froggy.

"Yeah, it's cool," said Ernie, somewhat embarrassed. "Let's call it a day. I don't know if I can survive another perfect wave."

It had been an excellent day for surfing. The waves, even the last one that ate Ernie, had been perfect, and sunbeams danced on the water as if on pogo sticks. Only a few late summer clouds, like fat lazy dragons, drifted through a simple, perfect Southern California sky.

As they pulled their surfboards from the water, Ernie spied something in the sand. "Dude," he said. "What's that?"

"What?" said Froggy.

"Over there. Is that a pig?"

"Well I believe it is," said Froggy. "And not a happy one at that."

Unhappy wasn't the half of it. The little pig was crying so hard she didn't even notice them approaching.

"Hey babe, why the tears?" said Ernie.

The little pig sat up, wiped the tears from her eyes and eyed the two of them with suspicion.

"Well," she said. "First, my name is not Babe.

Babe's that other pig—the one in the movies? And just because she's a big star, don't think she's better than me because she's not. I could like totally be in the movies too. If I wanted. Which I don't. And my name is Hoggy."

"Whoa, hold on little girl," said Froggy. "Ernie didn't mean anything by that. He calls all the girls babe."

"Well that is like such a bad habit and he should break it as soon as possible. It's totally uncool. And I'm not a little girl. As anyone can plainly see, I'm a pig."

And with that she broke down crying again, tears falling off her little pig cheeks onto the sand.

Froggy and Ernie looked at each other hardly knowing what to say. Finally, Froggy said, "But why are you so sad, Hoggy? It's such a beautiful day. An attractive pig like you should be happy."

"Well, if you must know," she said, "I'm probably going to be someone's supper. Something you probably know nothing about."

"Someone's supper?" Ernie again. "How is that possible?"

And with that the little pig composed herself and began the telling of her sad tale.

"You see", she said. "My father and mother are prize-winning pigs. They both won the blue ribbon at the State Fair last year. Then this year Mom and Dad were entered in the national competition. Of course Mom won the top prize again, beating even those stuck up pigs from Iowa. They think they're so hot cause they always win. But not this year. Mom was just too beautiful. This year California pigs ruled—or should have. But there was something fishy going on with the judges. The Governor of Iowa was even a judge. Like, how fair is that? He was a shifty, beady-eyed little man and I didn't trust him the minute I first saw him. Everyone said he never saw a bribe he didn't like. So Dad only came in second and as a reward for not taking the top prize he ended up being the main course at a Sunday barbeque."

"They ate him?" cried Froggy. "I can't believe it."

"Oh yeah," said Ernie. "I've seen it before. Happens all the time. If you're not numero uno, into the pot you go."

This, of course, wasn't true. No one in their right mind would eat a prize winning pig. They're much too valuable. Hoggy's father was missing because he had been loaned to a neighboring farmer for the purpose of, as they say, entertaining the ladies. But Hoggy was young, naïve, and unskilled in the ways of the world. She was convinced her dad had been eaten. So with that she broke down in tears again.

"Wait a minute," said Froggy. "That's very sad about your dad, but you have to get over it. They certainly aren't going to eat you."

"Don't be so sure," she said, fighting back the tears.

"This year they entered me in the competition at the County Fair. And I'll probably win. I mean, duh… look at me."

Froggy had to admit; she was a fine looking pig.

"Plus, I've got that whole talent portion of the contest like totally locked up. I can ride a bicycle standing on the seat on one leg. How many pigs can do that?"

"Yeah," said Ernie. "That should light the judges on fire… not."

Ignoring this, Hoggy continued. "But what if I don't win? What if someone bribes the judges again? It obviously happens like all the time. It's too terrible to think about. That's why I ran away. If only I could just fly away and pretend none of this is happening."

And with that her voice began to crack and she began to tremble. Uh oh, thought Ernie, here come the tears. But the tears didn't come. Instead, she sat up, cocked her head to the side and looked them up and down. Finally she said, "By the way, who are you anyway?"

CHAPTER 2

"Allow me to introduce myself," said Froggy. "My name is Froggy and this is my best friend and surfing buddy, Ernie."

Hoggy walked around him in a circle, looking him over.

"Well, with a name like Froggy, I'm guessing you're a frog. But you don't look like any frog I've ever seen. Frogs are like fat and round and lumpy and disgusting. And they're slimy and brown or grey."

And she was certainly right about that. Froggy was none of those things. He had smooth, deep-emerald green skin and long, muscular legs. He had a rather large, diamond-shaped head with a long, slender nose. In between each of his webbed toes was a circle of gold that perfectly matched the color of his eyeballs.

"No, no," he said. "You're thinking of the noble bull frog. A distant cousin of mine. I'm from the rain forest… Brazil, actually."

"Right. And I suppose if I kissed you, which is like so not going to happen, you would turn into a handsome prince."

Froggy laughed. "No, that's just a fairy tale, a myth, like getting warts if you touch a frog."

Yeah," said Ernie. "You can't get warts from a frog. Cooties maybe, but not warts."

"Cooties?" said Hoggy. "Eew!" And she quickly moved away from Froggy.

"Ernie's just kidding," said Froggy. "He does that."

"Well that's another bad habit. He seems to have quite a few," she said.

Hoggy then turned her attention to Ernie. "As for you, you're obviously some kind of bird, with wings and feathers and all. But I've never seen a bird quite like you either."

"Well," said Ernie. "That's because most people think I'm extinct. But there are a few of us still around. No thanks to the Tarahumara Indians in Mexico. That's where I'm from, Mexico. They seem to consider us a delicacy, as in they like to eat us? So I know a thing or two about relatives being eaten. In Mexico I'm referred to as an Imperial Woodpecker. With the emphasis on Imperial," he said quite proudly.

And, indeed, Ernie did look rather imperial. Standing almost two feet tall, he had white stripes running along the sides of his face and the length of his long, black-feathered body. He had a long, straight, white beak and tufts of bright-red feathers on either side of his head.

Boy, this guy sure is full of himself thought Hoggy. But she didn't say anything. Instead she said, "So what's with the sunglasses?"

Ernie was so used to wearing sunglasses that he sometimes forgot he even had them on.

Man, thought Ernie. This pig is so lame you have to explain everything to her.

"They're to keep the sun out of my eyes," he said quite abruptly.

Froggy sensed an argument brewing and he hated arguments. He was about to change the subject when Hoggy broke down in tears again.

"Oh, man. What now?" said Ernie.

"Well," she sobbed. "On top of everything else, I'm being stalked."

"Stalked?" said Ernie. "What do you mean stalked?"

"Jeez, Ernie, grab a clue. It means someone's following me."

"I *know* what it means. What *I* mean is…"

"We might be able to help," interrupted Froggy.

"Oh no," said Ernie. "No, no, no, no, no. No way, dude. That's not gonna happen. The last time you tried helping someone we almost ended up in jail."

"Why doesn't that surprise me?" said Hoggy. "Jail is probably where you both belong. The only surprise is…" She stopped mid-sentence and turned to Froggy.

"Did you say help?"

"Well, we have a friend," said Froggy.

Ernie thought about this for a second and decided this might not be such a bad idea after all. When they had problems, they always went to see Swami. If they went there now it would be Swami's problem and they could spend the rest of the summer surfing.

"Are you thinking Swami?" he said.

"Who else?" said Froggy.

"Who's Swami?" asked Hoggy.

"Just the guy they named this beach after," said Froggy.

"Well," she said. "I know this is called Swami's Beach but I didn't know there actually was a Swami."

"Yep," said Ernie. "And he lives close by. Let's go see what he has to say."

And, eager to have Swami tackle Hoggy's problem and leave him free to go surfing, Ernie led the way across the sand in search of Swami's house.

Froggy followed close behind and said, "Come on, Hoggy, it's not that far."

Before she could even think about it, Ernie and Froggy were off down the beach headed for the path that led up the steep bluff overlooking the water. Little did they know they were about to embark on an adventure that would take them deep into the heart of an ancient redwood forest hundreds of miles from home.

"Hey guys," she said. "Wait for me."

High on the cliff overlooking the beach, the bounty hunter known as Reacher stepped from the driver's side of a huge black Humvee. One shiny black boot, then the other, hit the hot asphalt. His left hand raised a pair of Vortex Viper Tactical binoculars to his mirrored sunglasses. He scanned the beach, locking in first on the pig, then the woodpecker, the frog, and finally back to the pig.

His right hand rested comfortably on the smooth mother of pearl handle of Calista, a safely sheathed, razor sharp, nine-inch titanium tipped dagger. It is said that once a dagger tastes blood it never forgets. If this is true there is much for Calista to remember. The bounty hunter known as Reacher had killed many times: animals, to be sure, but men as well. If there was trouble he would have to dispose of the frog and the woodpecker. A quick flash of blade would take care of that. But Calista wouldn't be tasting pig flesh today. In order to collect his reward he would have to bring the pig back alive.

CHAPTER 3

As they made their way through the ice plants, coastal sagewort and low saltbushes that lined the beach, Hoggy had a million questions.

"Who is this guy? Is he really a Swami? Why did they name a beach after him? How do you guys know him?"

"You'll see," was all they would say.

They continued until they came to a steep, rocky, narrow trail that climbed up the hill toward the top of the bluff. About half way up, the trail widened onto a flat area that revealed what appeared to be a deserted shack. Next to the shack stood a tall, lanky, middle-aged surfer waxing his surfboard and whistling to himself. Next to him an old blue tick hound lazed in the sun. When he saw Froggy and Ernie his tail began to move. Thump, thump, thump.

The surfer had long unkempt hair, tanned arms and legs, and was wearing baggy shorts, a torn T-shirt and flip-flops.

"Hey guys, 'sup?" he said without looking up. "Been out chasin' the Rhino?"

His back was turned to them and Hoggy wondered how he knew who they were or even that they were there at all.

"Dude," said Ernie. "It was awesome tubular. Went all jam up in a tumbler. Totally gnarly. Barely kicked out in time."

"That's not what I heard," said the surfer. "I heard that last tumbler planted you beak first in the sand. Froggy have to pull you out again?"

"Naw. It was cool," said Ernie. But he wasn't convincing anyone.

"Chasing the Rhino? Tumblers? What on earth are they talking about, Froggy?" said Hoggy.

"Don't pay any attention to that," said Froggy. "That's just surfer talk. Chasing the Rhino means looking for big waves."

The surfer then turned his attention to Hoggy. "So what's your problem, Hoggy?"

Hoggy could scarcely believe it. She had never met this… person before. Yet he knew her name and that she had a problem. How was that possible? And where was this Swami guy? Froggy, sensing her confusion, said, "Hoggy, I'd like you to meet Swami."

"You're Swami?" she said. "But you don't look like a Swami. You look more like, well, I don't know. You're just a surfer."

As soon as the words had escaped her little pig lips, the surfer instantly changed his appearance and transformed himself into a rather stately, white-robed, white-haired, white-bearded swami, complete with a fancy, colored wizard hat.

"Is this what you had in mind?" he teased.

Before she could respond he just as quickly changed into a pig, winking at Hoggy, then a frog, leaping over Froggy, and then he became a woodpecker and gave Ernie a high five. As she looked on in disbelief, he resumed his surfer image.

"We can be many things," he said. "But I'm way more comfortable looking like this."

"Swami can do some pretty cool stuff, huh?" said Ernie.

Hoggy couldn't believe what she was seeing. She felt as if she were in a dream. This can't possibly be real, she thought.

"Oh it's real alright," said Swami.

And he's reading my mind, too. It was all too much for her to take in. She felt weak and thought she might faint any second.

"Why don't you sit down," said Swami. "Maybe I can help."

Sitting down was exactly what she needed, and after a few moments she began to collect her thoughts, which she now knew were not entirely her own.

"As for your problem with winning the blue ribbon at the County Fair," he said, "I really can't help with that. I try to stay out of the affairs of others whenever possible. Who knows what would happen if I started fooling around with the judges' minds. Could get messy. And I don't do messy."

I knew it," she said. "No one can help me."

"Not so fast," said Swami. "I believe you mentioned something about flying away and pretending none of this is happening? Well I don't recommend pretending you don't have problems. They tend to catch up with you sooner or later. But as for the flying part, well that's no big deal. You could learn to fly, no problem."

"Oh sure," she said. "Haven't you ever heard the old saying 'that will happen when pigs fly.' It means it will like never happen, because pigs can't fly... and they never will."

"Well," he said, "if you're not interested, that's cool too."

"Wait a minute," said Froggy. "Are you saying she actually could learn to fly?"

Sure," said Swami. "Anyone can. Even you."

"Oh right," said Hoggy. "I suppose you just like sprout wings or something? I'd like to see that."

Swami laughed. "No, Hoggy. Wings aren't necessary. It's done with the most powerful tool you have. Your mind. You've heard the phrase 'thinking is the best way to travel'?

Well, it's true. Once you know the secret it's really quite simple. As Froggy and Ernie can tell you, I use this technique to fly myself."

"No way," said Hoggy, although at this point nothing would surprise her.

"Yes way," said Ernie. "I've seen it. But I didn't know anyone could do it. I thought you had to have, you know, like some special powers or something. Talk to me dude."

"No, Ernie, nothing special about it. But unfortunately I can't teach you myself," said Swami.

"I knew there was a catch," said Hoggy. "There always is."

"Now hold on Hoggy. I can't teach you, but I know someone who can. And I just might be able to persuade him to take on some new students."

"That is so cool," said Ernie. "Does he live around here?"

"Unfortunately, no. He lives deep in the forest in a place called Big Sur. Quite a distance from here, but that should be no problem for a couple of enterprising guys like you."

Ernie pulled an iPhone out of its waterproof pouch. Ernie never went anywhere, even surfing, without his iPhone. He did a MapQuest search for Big Sur.

"429.54 miles," he said. "Estimated travel time seven hours, forty-two minutes. Piece of cake."

"Yeah," said Hoggy. "And I suppose you like have a car?"

"Nope, but Louise will get us there," said Ernie.

"Louise? Who's Louise?"

"You'll see," said Ernie.

While all this was going on Swami was giving Froggy all the information they would need once they reached Big Sur. He was, of course, doing so telepathically so Hoggy and Ernie heard not a thing.

Even though Ernie didn't hear any of this, he knew how things worked with Swami. He looked at Froggy and said, "Got everything we need?"

"Yep," said Froggy.

"Good, then let's go get Louise."

And off they went down the trail that led away from Swami's shack.

"Hey, guys, wait for me," said Hoggy.

The bounty hunter known as Reacher adjusted the volume on his Bose 3-band equalizer frequency headset. The six panel Monster Ear Sound Amplifier was pointed at Swami's shack from his position on the cliff above. He had heard the entire conversation. So they're going north to Big Sur, he thought. Well, if there were too many people around, maybe the open road would be a better place to take the pig. He had plenty of time and this had to be done right. If any do-gooder witnesses decided to call the police he would have a lot of explaining to do. There was a warrant out for his arrest in three states.

CHAPTER 4

Once they reached the beach they did the low tide rock dance, skipping and hopping from rock to rock through tide pools teeming with sea anemones and starfish, until they reached the rickety old wooden stairs that climbed back up the cliff. At the top of the stairs was a small park with a statue of Swami. They made their way through the park and down an alley that ended in a Starbuck's parking lot.

"There she is," said Ernie. "What do you think? Pretty cool, huh?"

Hoggy looked around the parking lot but didn't see anyone. All she saw were about a dozen cars and what looked like a motorcycle, but not really, because it had three wheels.

"What are your talking about?" she said. "There's no one here. Where's Louise?"

"You're standing right next to her," said Ernie.

Hoggy looked around again and then she saw it. She was standing next to a bright canary-yellow, three-wheeled motorcycle and on the right rear bumper, in candy-apple-red and very fancy script was the word “Louise”.

“This is Louise?” said Hoggy. “We’re going to travel over 400 miles on a tricycle?”

“Not a tricycle,” said Ernie indignantly. “It’s a motorcycle, a genuine Harley.”

“Harley?” said Hoggy.

“Duh. As in Harley Davidson. Only the finest motorcycle ever made.”

“I hate to disappoint you, Ernie, but this is not a motorcycle. It has like three wheels, which makes it a tricycle.”

“Whatever,” said Ernie. “But I can assure you she will definitely get us to Big Sur. She’s got an air cooled, twin cam, 103-engine that tops out at over 130 miles per hour.”

“If you think I’m getting on a tricycle that goes 130 miles an hour, you have completely lost your mind. That is if you ever had one,” she said.

“Ernie never actually got it up to 130,” said Froggy. “But he could if he wanted to. We never go over the speed limit,” he said, trying to sound responsible. “Louise is a Tri-Glide Ultra Classic and has been customized. The seat’s been raised and moved forward to accommodate Ernie’s short wing span.”

“Whatever,” said Hoggy. But she did have to admit this—whatever it was—did look pretty cool. She liked the bright-yellow paint and all the glistening chrome. And there was more than enough room behind the driver's seat for a frog and a pig.

"Well, I don't know," she said. "Is it like safe?"

"Never been raced, rolled or wrecked," said Ernie. "I'm a very careful driver."

"So," said Froggy, "it's all settled. We just need to get you a helmet."

Froggy opened the rear storage compartment and, where there were normally two helmets, found a third.

"Must be Swami's doing," he said as he handed Hoggy a brand new helmet with "Hoggy" written on the side. It was even her favorite color, pink.

"Uh oh," said Froggy. "Look at this." He pulled a paper flyer from the windshield of the car parked next to Louise. On it was a picture of Hoggy with the caption:

"Lost Pig – $50,000 Reward"

"If there really is someone following you, this is the reason." said Froggy. "They're after the reward."

"Whoa," said Ernie. "Fifty big ones. They must really want you back."

"Only fifty thousand?" said Hoggy, a little disappointed. "I thought it would be more."

"Well, no matter how much it is, they're looking for you, Hoggy. We better get out of here fast," said Froggy.

"Let's do it," cried Hoggy as she and Froggy piled into the rear seat.

"Next stop, Los Angeles," said Ernie. "We're gonna learn how to fly."

What does he mean *we*, thought Hoggy. But she didn't say anything.

As they started to pull out of the parking lot Ernie stopped abruptly. Parked on the other side of the lot was the black Hummer and standing next to it was Reacher, dressed entirely in black, his hand resting on the dagger, a wicked smile on his cruel face.

"That's him!" cried Hoggy.

"Who?" said Froggy.

"The guy who's been following me. That's him!"

Ernie put Louise back in drive, hit the gas, popped a wheelie and left ten feet of Michelin rubber on the asphalt as they raced from the parking lot.

So much for driving safely, thought Hoggy.

Reacher didn't even blink. He knew where they were going and he knew the three-wheeled motorcycle could easily outrun his clunky Hummer. He would take the pig when the time was right and not before. It would be a little more difficult now that they knew who he was but that would only make the game that much more interesting.

PART TWO

THE TRIP

CHAPTER 5

About an hour and a half later it was starting to get dark as they made their way up Laurel Canyon, one of the many canyons that connect Los Angeles with the San Fernando Valley. They were headed for the famous Mulholland Drive when Froggy asked, "Ever been to Los Angeles, Hoggy?"

"I was born two miles from Swami's Beach, Froggy. And the beach is as far away from home as I ever got."

"Well, you're in for a surprise. They call Paris the *City of Lights*, but Paris has nothing on Los Angeles."

When they reached the top of the canyon, Ernie steered Louise left at Mulholland Drive and pulled into a small parking area. Hoggy couldn't believe her eyes. There were city lights as far as the eye could see. On one side was the San Fernando Valley and on the other the Los Angeles basin. The lights seemed to go on forever, stopping only when they reached the sea. She had never seen so many lights. It was as if someone had plucked the Milky Way from the sky and set it down on land.

They decided that someone should stay awake to be on the look out for the stalker so Ernie volunteered for the first shift. Froggy and Hoggy unrolled their sleeping bags, which had somehow appeared in Louise's storage compartment—Swami again—and went to sleep under the stars with Hoggy dreaming about pigs flying.

The next morning Ernie checked the GPS app on his iPhone.

"We have two options," he said. "We can take the inland route, which is the fastest, or we can take the coastal route which is totally cool."

"Inland," said Hoggy. "We don't want to waste any time."

"Inland it is," said Froggy.

"Let's roll," said Ernie.

So off they went down Mulholland Drive west to the San Diego Freeway, then North to the I-5. But as they left the San Fernando Valley, Ernie felt something funny in Louise's steering. He pulled off to the side of the highway and stopped.

"What now?" asked Hoggy rather impatiently.

"I don't know. Something's not right with the steering," said Ernie.

They sat in silence for a few moments as Ernie jumped off Louise and began to examine her front wheel. Then they heard it. And felt it too. It started out as a low rumble like distant thunder or a far away freight train. Louise rolled forward a few inches. Then back. The rumble became louder and the earth began to gently roll beneath their feet making it difficult to stand. It wasn't Louise's steering at all. It was an earthquake!

A crack appeared in the highway right next to Hoggy, and as it widened she lost her balance and started to fall backwards into it.

Froggy reached out and grabbed her by the snout, pulling her away from the collapsing earth. And just in time too, because what followed was beyond imagination. The earth was in pain and began screaming. An ear splitting CRACK . . . BOOM . . . CRACK echoed through the air like a jet breaking the sound barrier, only louder. The crack where Hoggy had been standing opened as the ground groaned and shook. Froggy was launched into the air and Ernie was catapulted over Louise, landing on his head, sunglasses flying off to the side. Hoggy was hanging on to Louise for her very life.

Then silence. It was over. Just like that, it ended as quickly as it had begun. It lasted less than a minute, but seemed like an hour.

Ernie got up, dusted himself off, found his sunglasses, and began to survey the damage. Louise seemed to be okay but Hoggy was shaking so bad you would have thought the earthquake hadn't yet stopped. But she was the least of his problems. At least she was safe, which was more than he could say for Froggy. The crack that Froggy had saved Hoggy from falling into was no longer just a crack in the pavement. It was now a giant rupture in the earth more than twenty feet wide. The far side of the rupture had sunk and was now at least fifteen feet below where Ernie stood.

He looked into a divide that could have been the Devil's own volcano. Clouds of dust, like coiled snakes, bellowed from the gaping pit. And there, on the other side, was his pal Froggy.

"Dude," he said. "You okay?"

"I think so. But there seems to be a small space between us."

"This is straight-up whack," said Ernie. "I'm talkin' serious bad berries here."

"How far do you think it is?" said Froggy. Ernie quickly moved to Louise's storage compartment, removed a laser tape measure, pointed it at the other side and pushed a button. A laser beam streaked out to the far side, sending a signal back. He immediately got a digital readout.

"Twenty-three feet, nine inches," he said.

"Wow," said Froggy. "That would be a world record."

"Indeed it would, my brother. Think you're up to it?"

"Well, I guess we'll soon find out," said Froggy.

Hoggy finally composed herself and had stopped shaking. She and Ernie watched as Froggy padded back and forth trying to focus on the task at hand. He had never jumped twenty-three feet, nine inches before. Could he do it? Yes, he decided, it could be done.

“Come on, Froggy, you can do it,” cried Hoggy.

“Remember Calaveras County,” coaxed Ernie.

And with that, Froggy eyed the other side that would be his landing space, reared back on his powerful hind legs, let out a Ninja scream and launched himself into the air. About half way into his flight, however, Froggy realized the truth. It was too far. He wasn't going to make it.

He began furiously pumping his legs as if bicycling in midair and reached out with his long arms in a desperate attempt to reach his goal. But instead of landing safely on his feet, he found himself hanging from the cliff like a fish on a line.

Now normally this would not have been a problem. Tree frogs are excellent climbers and had the cliff been straight up and down, he could have easily climbed to safety. But the cliff was more like an overhang and he couldn't find a foothold to pull himself out.

Ernie ran down to help his friend out of danger. He reached out with one wing but every time Froggy grabbed on, Ernie began slipping toward the edge himself. Not only was the cliff an overhang, it wasn't flat either. It sloped down at an angle and Ernie couldn't get a good grip on the ground.

“Back Louise up to the edge,” cried Hoggy.

“Good idea,” said Ernie as he scampered to ready Louise for the rescue. He backed Louise down the cliff but couldn't get close enough to the edge. The quake had left too much debris and there were large rocks blocking the way.

"Pull forward," said Hoggy. As Ernie eased Louise away from the cliff's edge, Hoggy hopped on the back, hooked her tail to the handle of the storage compartment and hung her little pig body out over Louise's rear bumper.

"Now back up," she said.

"Are you crazy?" said Ernie. "It'll never work."

"Just do it, Ernie."

Ernie slowly backed up to the cliff's edge and Hoggy was able to get close enough to reach out for Froggy.

"Go ahead, Froggy. Grab my arm."

"No way," said Froggy. "I'll pull you off and we'll both go down."

Now there are a couple of things most people don't know about pigs. Number one is that the strongest part of their body is their tail. It's hard as a boiled owl and strong as ironwood. As Ernie would later say, "Wasn't nothin' gonna pull Hoggy off that Harley. Louise's bumper would have fallen off before Hoggy's tail gave out."

Number two is they are fiercely determined. Once they make up their mind about something that's the end of the conversation.

Very calmly, almost whispering, she said, "Froggy, I don't want to argue about this. Take hold of my arm."

"I don't know, Hoggy."

"JUST DO IT, FROGGY!" she screamed.

"Okay, okay."

He reached out and, dangling by one hand, took hold of her arm with the other. She glanced back at Ernie.

"Okay, move forward."

Ernie put Louise in drive and began to inch forward. At first Louise slipped on the loose rock but gradually found traction and was able to pull Froggy to safety.

Hoggy unhooked her tail and ran to Froggy. She jumped up and gave him a big kiss right on the end of his green nose.

"Oh Froggy, you're safe. You made it."

"Thanks to you, Hoggy. You saved my life."

Hoggy began to blush, which isn't easy for a pig since her face was mostly pink anyway.

"We couldn't have done it without Ernie and Louise," she said. They looked over to see Ernie taking a rather theatrical bow.

"By the way," said Ernie. "I don't know if you noticed, but when you kissed Froggy, which, if I recall, was so not going to happen, he didn't turn into a handsome prince. And you didn't get warts either. I would check myself for cooties though."

"Oh shut up, Ernie," she said.

But she was giggling and he could tell she didn't really mean it.

At first Ernie thought he might be able to maneuver Louise around the great divide that had split the I-5. But as he surveyed the situation, it became clear that they were not going to continue north. The divide went as far as the eye could see, both east and west.

"We have to turn around," he said.

"I knew it," said Hoggy. "We'll never make it. I don't know why we ever started out in the first place."

"Hold on, Hoggy. We have to turn around, but we don't have to turn back." He was looking at his GPS.

"If we go back seven miles we can cut over to the coast. It takes a little longer, but we'll make it. Just adds some extra time."

"You mean it, Ernie? That is like so awesome."

"Plan B," said Froggy. "Always have a Plan B." As they were collecting their things that had been thrown from Louise's storage compartment, Hoggy thought of something.

"What was all that stuff about Calaveras County and world records?"

"It's nothing," said Froggy. "Hardly worth mentioning."

"Hardly worth mentioning?" said Ernie. "Dude, you're way too modest."

"What in the world are you two talking about now?" said Hoggy.

"Why don't you drive," said Ernie. "I'll sit in the back and tell Hoggy the story."

"Ernie, it's not a big deal," said Froggy.

"I want to know," said Hoggy. "You drive."

So Froggy, outnumbered, slid into the driver's seat while Ernie and Hoggy piled in behind.

"Next stop, Big Sur," said Ernie. "We're gonna learn to fly."

There, he said it again, thought Hoggy. *We*. But she didn't say anything as they put on their helmets and headed south to find the nearest short cut to the coast.

CHAPTER 6

Once they were on their way, Ernie began his story. "You see," he said. "About a year ago…". But before he could continue Froggy pulled Louise over to the side of the road.

"What now?" said Hoggy. She was getting very tired of all the interruptions.

Froggy pointed up the road saying nothing. About a hundred yards away was the black Hummer, its front and back right side wheels stuck in a ditch created by the earthquake. It leaned at a forty five degree angle and looked as if it might tip over any second. The bounty hunter was nowhere to be seen.

“Maybe he’s dead,” said Ernie.

But as soon as he said it the driver's side door opened and Reacher pulled himself out. As he hopped to the ground the Hummer tilted ever so slightly to starboard and slowly toppled into the ditch, all four wheels pointed skyward like a capsized sand tortoise baking in the sun.

"Go for it," said Ernie as Froggy hit the gas and sent Louise screaming down the highway. They were doing ninety when they passed the Hummer and Reacher dived into the ditch as they raced by.

"So much for driving safely," said Hoggy.

"You gotta do what you gotta do," said Ernie. "I told you Louise would get us there." He sounded like a proud parent.

As he watched them disappear down the highway, Reacher dusted himself off, pulled an iPhone from the pocket of his black leather vest and hit speed dial for emergency road side service. This was getting more complicated than he anticipated.

Once safely on their way Ernie continued his story.

"As I was saying, about a year ago Froggy and me, we're jonesin' for some…"

"Jonesing?" said Hoggy. "What's jonesing?"

"You know, like, we had this, I don't know, this sort of craving for…"

"Well why didn't you just say so, Ernie? Why don't you just like speak English? Is that so hard?"

If you had been able to see behind Ernie's sunglasses you would have seen him rolling his eyes. This is going to be a long trip, he thought. But he didn't say anything.

"Okay, okay. We had this, uh, strong desire for some fresh artichokes and since…"

"Artichokes?" said Hoggy. "I love artichokes. I was like practically raised on artichokes. I remember one time I was like really young and… "

Ernie removed his sunglasses, which he never did, and fixed her with a hard stare. "Hoggy, do you want to hear this story or not?"

"Sorry. I'm just saying… never mind. Go ahead."

"As I was saying, we had this, uh, strong desire for some fresh artichokes. Since we were only about a hundred miles from Castroville, which just happens to be the artichoke capital of the world, we thought we'd head over for a feast. On the way we were passing through Calaveras County when we saw a sign that said Frogtown. Well, we could hardly pass up a town with a name like that, so we took a short detour to check it out.

"Turns out, every year they have a celebration called the 'Jumping Frog Jubilee of Calaveras County'. Sort of like a County Fair. And the main attraction is a jumping frog contest. I mean this is like the Super Bowl of frog jumping. Frogs come from all over the world to compete.

"Now I've seen Froggy jump. Can't nobody touch Froggy when it comes to jumping. So I talked him into entering the contest. Seems the world record for this contest was twenty-one feet, five and three-quarter inches set back in 1986 by a frog known as Rosie the Ribiter. Ha. I've see Froggy jump twenty-two feet without even trying so this was gonna be a piece of cake. Like shootin' fish in a teacup.

"Anyway, we got Froggy registered and the way it works is each frog has what they call a jockey. But the jockeys don't actually ride the frogs. They just get 'em lined up at the starting line and tell 'em when it's time to jump.

"By the time it was Froggy's turn, the best jump of the day was by a California Red Legged Frog named 4Peat. Local kid. Kinda scrawny if you ask me, and cocky too. Acted like he owned the place. Struttin' all around like 'Hey, look at me… I'm the Dude.' Yeah, right. His best jump was nineteen feet, eleven inches. What a joke. You've seen Froggy jump. Ol' 4Peat didn't stand a chance.

"So Froggy steps up to the starting line and I'm telling ya', he was dialed in."

"I'm going to assume that means he was like ready?" said Hoggy.

"Ready and then some. Anyway, I get the signal from the judge and relay it to Froggy, and he rears back on those long legs of his, takes a deep breath and takes off. It was spectacular. The crowd had never seen anything like it. There was total silence as Froggy flew, and flew, and flew. Seemed like he'd never come down. When he finally landed the judges couldn't believe their eyes: twenty-three feet, eight inches.

A new world record. He beat the old record by more than two feet, and beat old 4Peat by three and a half feet.

"The crowd went crazy. The band began to play and people poured out of the stands to congratulate him. One young girl rushed onto the court, put Froggy on her shoulders and went dancing through the crowd. Froggy was like a hero. You've never seen anything like it. Everyone said it was something they would tell their grandchildren. 'I was there the day Froggy set the record'.

"But then the celebration was interrupted by an announcement over the loud speaker. Seems that ol' 4Peat's jockey got his panties in a bunch. He didn't take very kindly to defeat and had lodged a protest with the judges. He claimed the jockey had to be human and Froggy should be disqualified because his jockey was a woodpecker!

"So the judges went inside a small tent to review the instant replay on their video monitors and to check the rule book. After about ten minutes they came out of the tent and the Head Judge took the microphone.

"After further review it is the decision of the judges that because Froggy's jockey is not human, he be disqualified. The winner is 4Peat with a jump of nineteen feet, eleven inches.

"Well I thought there was going to be a riot. The air was filled with boos as people poured back onto the court from the stands. The judges had to be escorted to their cars by State Troopers. There was total chaos so Froggy and I jumped on Louise and jammed out of there fast.

"And that's how Froggy became the real life version of 'Mark Twain's Celebrated Jumping Frog of Calaveras County'. People still talk about it today.

"No matter what the record book says, Froggy owns that record. Froggy is *The Man*… or in this case, *The Frog*."

Froggy was pulling into a gas station just as Ernie was finishing his story. When they stopped Hoggy jumped into the driver's seat and gave Froggy a big hug.

"Oh, Froggy. You're my hero. You're the world champion jumper."

Froggy started to blush a deep yellow, which is what you get when you mix red and green.

When they had finished gassing up, they piled back on Louise and Ernie said, "Come on guys, we're gonna learn how to fly."

There, he said it again, thought Hoggy. *We*. She could no longer contain herself.

"You keep saying *we're* gonna learn how to fly. But Froggy and I are the ones who are gonna learn. You already know how to fly, being a bird and all. You must just be excited for us, right?"

"Well, I mean… you know… yeah, that's it. I'm excited for you."

"Come on, Ernie," said Froggy. "You might as well tell her. She's going to find out sooner or later anyway."

"Find out what?" said Hoggy.

“It’s nothing,” said Ernie.

“If you don’t tell her, I will,” said Froggy.

“What? Tell me what?” said Hoggy.

“Okay, okay,” said Ernie. “It’s just that, well, I never did, you know, I never actually…”

”Ernie!” said Froggy.

“I can’t fly,” whispered Ernie.

“What?” said Hoggy.

“I said I can’t fly. There. Are you happy now? I never learned.”

“What do you mean you can’t fly. Of course you can fly. You’re a bird.”

“Ernie, why don’t you drive and I’ll explain everything to Hoggy,” said Froggy.

So Ernie slumped into the driver’s seat while Froggy and Hoggy got in behind as Louise set off again for Big Sur.

CHAPTER 7

"You see, Hoggy, as Ernie already told you, he's from Mexico. He was born in a forest in the mountains outside a town called San Miguel de Allende in Central Mexico. A few days after he was hatched, when he barely had his eyes open, he was sitting in his nest with two brothers and a sister waiting for his mom to bring them lunch. His dad was perched higher up the tree keeping an eye out for any pesky Tarahumara who might be lurking about. Ernie wasn't kidding when he said the Tarahumara were fond of eating Imperial Woodpeckers. They especially like nestlings like Ernie and his brothers and sister.

"As Ernie's dad was keeping watch, he noticed quite a commotion at the bottom of the tree. He couldn't figure out what was going on but decided it couldn't be too bad, since the disturbance was brought by men but not the dreaded Tarahumara. The men were behaving oddly as they fastened ropes and chains to the different parts of the trees.

Then, without warning, there came a terrible noise from the machines they carried. They began attacking the trees as if they were mortal enemies and one by one the trees began to fall. All through the forest, trees were falling everywhere. The sound was more than Ernie could bear.

"Then the tree in which Ernie's nest rested began to fall as well. Frantically, Ernie's dad tried to catch the nest as the tree swayed back and forth, but it happened so fast he was unable to catch the falling nest. All four hatchlings went flying through the air and crashed to the ground, other trees falling all around them.

"That was the last thing Ernie remembered. He was knocked unconscious by the branch of another tree.

"Two days later, when Ernie awoke, he looked into what he would remember as the softest, kindest eyes he would ever see. But it wasn't his mom. These eyes were human."

"He's awake," she said. "Hi there, little guy."

"Ernie had no idea who this person was but he felt somehow safe, for she had a smile that would light up an Iowa cornfield in summer."

"Where's my mom and dad?" he said. "And my brothers and sister? And who are you?"

"My name is Ximena," she said. "And there's plenty of time to explain everything, but right now we have to concentrate on getting you well."

"Ernie tried to prop himself up to look around only to find that he couldn't move his right wing."

"What's that?" he asked, looking at some wood attached to his wing.

"Oh, those are popsicle sticks. I used them as a splint. You, my young friend, have a broken wing. But that's enough for now. You get some rest and we'll talk later."

"The next few weeks were spent bringing Ernie back to health. Ximena fed him every day and, when his wing had healed, she made him exercise it so that it would be strong enough for him to fly.

"She explained to him that some very bad men had come into the forest to cut down all the trees. Not just some of the trees, but all."

"Why would they do that?" he asked.

"For money, Ernie. They have no regard for the animals and birds or for the soil erosion caused by their stupidity. They think only of money!"

"She also explained to him that, unfortunately, his father had not survived the experience. He had been hit by a falling tree as he tried to save the four hatchlings. His brothers and sister had also perished. As for his mother, Ximena didn't know what to say. They had searched and searched, but she was nowhere to be found. So now it was just Ernie. No parents. No brothers or sister. Alone."

As Hoggy listened to the story, tears started to form in her little pig eyes.

"Oh, Froggy. That is so sad. I had no idea. Poor Ernie. But why didn't he learn how to fly? Was it his wing?"

"Well," said Froggy. "That was part of it. Over the years Ximena taught Ernie a great deal. She taught him to read and write and she also taught him five languages. I bet you didn't know Ernie could speak five languages did you?"

"Five?"

"Yep. English, Spanish, French, Portuguese and Sanskrit. Ximena was fond of saying that only Americans spoke one language."

"What's Sanskrit? I never heard of that."

"Sanskrit is the ancient language of India. Ximena is as practical as anyone you might meet but when she was younger she traveled far and wide. She ended up in India where she spent several years with a holy man. For all her practicality, she is well versed in meditation as well as yoga.

"But try as she might, she could never figure out how to teach a bird to fly. I guess that's something only your mom can teach you. So Ernie grew up walking everywhere he went. Needless to say he was pretty bummed out. He was probably the only bird on the planet that couldn't fly.

"One day when Ernie returned home after a long walk he noticed something new parked next to the house—a bright yellow, three-wheeled motorcycle."

"How do you like it?" asked Ximena.

"What is it?"

"It's your new set of wheels. If you can't fly, at least you won't have to walk."

"No way. For me? That is so cool. You got this for me?"

"Yes, and now you have to name it. Every motorcycle has to have a name. So what will it be?"

"Without even thinking, Ernie said, 'Louise'. That was my mom's name. Louise."

"Louise it is," said Ximena as she pulled a stool up to the motorcycle and unpacked her paints.

"You see Hoggy, Ximena was quite a famous artist and minutes later 'Louise' was written in bright, candy-apple-red script on the side of the motorcycle.

"With his new found mobility, Ernie decided to set out in search for his mom. He spent the next several months traveling all over Mexico. First south, then east, north and finally west and back home to San Miguel de Allende and his adopted mother, Ximena. But his real mom was nowhere to be found and he was about ready to give up his search when Ximena suggested he go farther north. Maybe even to the United States."

"Who knows," she said. "Maybe she somehow made it out of Mexico. I have a friend named Swami who might be able to help you."

"So Ernie said goodbye to Ximena and set his sights on North America. Several weeks later he found himself in Encinitas at Swami's Beach. That's where I met him.

"And that, Hoggy, is how you came to be riding a three-wheeled motorcycle with a woodpecker that can't fly."

"Wow," was all she could say.

They had pulled into another gas station as Froggy was finishing his story and Ernie was stretching his legs and checking the GPS on his iPhone.

Now you've probably never seen a pig hugging a woodpecker (who has?). But that's exactly what was happening in the parking lot of that gas station.

"What was that for?" asked Ernie.

"Just because."

"Oh, okay. Well, thanks, I guess. But now that you know my secret, try to keep it yourself. It's not good for my image."

Somewhat embarrassed, Ernie quickly changed the subject.

"We have officially entered the Big Sur area and according to the coordinates Swami gave us, we're only about eight miles from the Big Sur Inn. That's where we're supposed to find someone named Calliope Rose. She's gonna tell us how to find Swami's friend, some dude named Stokes."

So they piled back on Louise and continued north.

PART THREE

CALLIOPE ROSE AND THE PATH

CHAPTER 8

Froggy and Hoggy had been so engrossed in the story that they really hadn't been paying attention to their surroundings. But now they watched in silent awe at the beauty of Big Sur unfolding before them.

On their left the purple mountains dropped straight down into the sea. They passed over the Bixby Bridge, which spans Rainbow Canyon, a giant gorge that meanders onto the rugged coastline below. There are no beaches in this area, only 100-foot cliffs overlooking huge jagged rocks rising out of the ocean like sea creatures.

As they approached the town of Big Sur, the green and purple mountains gave way to pine forests that stretched all the way to the sea. Then, as they continued, the pine forests abruptly disappeared and they got their first glimpse of the tallest trees in the world. The giant Redwood Sequoias of Big Sur, California.

Ernie pulled Louise to the side of the road and they stood, astonished, looking up at these giants that reached two-hundred, two-hundred fifty, three-hundred feet into the clear Big Sur sky.

Imagine a tree as tall as a thirty-story building and twenty feet across at the base. Some of these trees had been standing sentinel over the rugged coastline for two thousand years. Even Ernie, who was rarely at a loss for words, viewed the scene in silence.

Finally, after several minutes, Hoggy broke the spell they seemed to be under.

"Awesome," was all she could say.

"Awesome indeed," said Froggy. Then, always the practical one, "But we're almost there so let's get going."

They jumped back on Louise and started out again, but this time much slower. Everything seemed to slow down in the presence of these ancient giants.

A few minutes later Ernie again stopped at the side of the road next to what looked like a small cottage. Off to the right were several smaller cabins.

"According to the GPS coordinates Swami gave us we should be there."

But as they looked around they didn't see anything that looked like it might be an Inn.

"Maybe someone lives here," said Froggy pointing to the small cottage.

"Let's see if they know where to find the Inn."

The cobblestone path leading to the cottage was made of river stones collected from the Big Sur River that passed through the forest on its way to the sea. The cottage itself was made of larger river stones and had two chimneys poking out from a sharply pitched roof. There was a wooden front door painted blue and as they approached they could see a small wooden plaque above the door. Etched into the sign they read:

Within these sacred portals
Revenge and Hate must cease.
The souls of straying mortals
In love will find release.

"Wow," said Ernie. "That's heavy stuff. Whoever lives here must be pretty far out.

"Mozart," said Froggy.

"Mozart?" said Hoggy and Ernie in unison.

"Yep, Mozart. It's from an opera called The Magic Flute. Dates back to about 1700." Now Ernie was used to this kind of thing from Froggy. After all they had been friends for quite some time. But Hoggy was still amazed by all the things Froggy knew.

"How do you like know all this stuff, Froggy?" she asked.

Ernie answered for him. "He reads a lot. Plus, he went to college," he said, quite proud to have a friend who went to college.

"College?" said Hoggy. "You went to college? How cool."

"Yeah, but that's another story," said Froggy. "Right now we have to find the Inn.

So they knocked on the door, but no one answered. They knocked louder. Still no answer. Then Froggy noticed the door was slightly ajar so he nudged it open ever so slightly and peeked in.

"You gonna stand out there all day?" came a voice from within. They took a few steps inside and could see someone standing behind what looked like a small desk. On closer inspection they could see that it was a woman. A tall woman. Very tall. Taller even than Swami. She had long red hair tied back in a braid and bright, sea-green eyes. She was wearing faded jeans and a T-shirt that proclaimed ZZTop across the front.

"What can I do for you?" she said.

Ernie hopped up on the desk.

"We're kind of jammed up," he said.

"If by jammed up you mean lost, why don't you just say so?"

"Uh, okay, we're lost then. We're trying to find the Big Sur Inn."

"Well congratulations."

"Pardon me?" said Ernie.

"No need to pardon you. Unless you've done something you weren't supposed to. You haven't, have you?"

"Well, ah, no… but why congratulate me?"

"Because you found it," she said.

"Found what?" Ernie was getting confused by this time.

"The Big Sur Inn, of course."

"This is it?"

"Do you have some kind of hearing impairment?" she said.

"No, it's just that… never mind. If this is the Big Sur Inn, then we're looking for Calliope Rose," he said.

"Good for you," she said.

"Well, do you know where we can find her?"

"Sure do." Silence.

"Well, are you going to tell me?"

"Tell you what?"

"Where we can find Calliope Rose."

"You're looking at her."

"Why didn't you say so?"

"I just did."

Ernie was really getting confused now.

“I’m glad we got that out of the way. Can you tell us how to find Stokes?”

“I thought you were looking for Calliope Rose.”

“Yeah, but she knows where Stokes is.”

“Okay.”

“Well, do you know where he is?”

“Nope. Never heard of him. If it is a him. Could be a girl for all I know.”

“There must be some mistake.”

“I’m sure there is. From the looks of you, I’m sure you make a lot of mistakes. And often, too.”

“Let me try this,” said Froggy.

“Well,” she said. “I hope you’re smarter than your friend here. He’s not too bright now is he?”

“Now wait a minute,” said Ernie. He’d had just about enough of her abuse.

“Hold on,” said Froggy. “I’ll handle this.” He looked Calliope Rose up and down and very quietly, almost whispering, repeated the instructions he had received from Swami.

“Rama Lama Ding Dong.”

“Bop Shu Bop,” she said.

“Doo Wah Ditty,” said Froggy.

And with that little exchange Calliope Rose underwent an attitude adjustment.

"Nice to make your acquaintance, Froggy. You too, Ernie. And you must be Hoggy. What took you so long? I expected you hours ago."

At this point Hoggy could contain herself no longer.

"Stop. Stop. Stop," she said. "What's going on here? What's with all the secrecy and the Bop Ditty Ding Dong or whatever that was? And how come everyone knows what's going on except me? How do you like know our names?"

"Now Hoggy," said Calliope Rose. "Don't get your little pig snout in an uproar. It's really quite simple. I know your names cause Swami told me."

"Swami?" said Hoggy.

"Yep. You just missed him. He left about an hour ago. Said you were headed this way. As for the secrecy, well, a body can't be too careful these days. For all I know you coulda been Rakshasas, poking your filthy noses into Stokes' business. Askin' all kinds of questions. But Froggy here knew the code words and he could only have learned that from Swami. Swami also told me why you were late. Got hung up in an earthquake, did ya? Nasty business those earthquakes. You ask me a body's gotta be plumb crazy to live down South."

"Well, okay," said Hoggy. "Like I'm sorry. But there's so much weird stuff going on. And what's this about Rakshasas asking about Stokes? I never heard of Rakshasas. And why would they be looking for Stokes? Are they like the police? Is Stokes like wanted for something? It would be just my luck that we traveled all this way looking for a criminal."

Calliope Rose just laughed.

"Good lord no, child. Stokes ain't no criminal. Far from it. As for them Rakshasas, I'll fill ya'll in on that later. Right now we're gonna have some nice lunch and then you can rest up some. You must be plumb tuckered out and worn to a frazzle from your ride.

"By the way, Louise is pretty as a picture. Even prettier than I imagined, Ernie."

"Here we go again," cried Hoggy. "How could you possibly know about Louise? Oh…", she stopped to think about it. "I forgot, Swami probably told you."

"Actually," said Calliope Rose, "Swami never mentioned it. Ximena told me about Louise a few years back. Now before you go gettin' all crazy on me, let me just say that Ximena and I are old friends. I met her in Mexico right after Ernie headed north on Louise way back when. She told me all about him bein' a orphan and all.

"But right now let's eat. I'm hungrier than a woodpecker with a headache. No offense, Ernie."

CHAPTER 9

After lunch Calliope Rose gathered everyone around a large table in the dining room of the Inn. The other guests had departed so they had the room to themselves.

"Okay," she said. "If you're gonna find Stokes there's a few things you gotta know. First of all it ain't gonna be easy. He don't live too far from here, maybe three, four days walk. Some say nine or ten days. Nobody really knows for sure. Far as I know nobody round these parts has actually been there. Now I can point you in the right direction but after that you're on your own.

"Secondly, you gotta know 'bout them Rakshasas. Those dudes are nothin' to mess around with. Some of 'em ain't too smart. Wouldn't know their butt from a large moon crater. But their leaders are not only smart, but clever too. They're shape changers and illusionists. They can take any form they want in order to trick you. They can even possess you if it suits their purpose. They have super human strength, are mean as jackals, and they ain't afraid of nothin'. Oh, and did I mention they like to eat humans? They got no culinary skills at all so they don't cook 'em either. They just eat 'em alive.

"And even though humans would be their first choice for dinner, I'm sure they wouldn't pass up a nice succulent pig. Or a frog for that matter. Ernie, you might survive cause they detest birds. And the feelin's mutual. Birds won't go anywhere near a forest occupied by Rakshasas. That's how you can tell if you're in a forest where there's Rakshasas hangin' out. Not a bird in sight.

"And ugly? You think you've seen ugly? They got long pointed teeth and eyes like zombies. Some of 'em are ten, twelve feet tall and their arms hang almost to the ground. Some are so hairy they look like big ol' apes while others are completely hairless. Hard to say which one looks worse. And their fingernails, which sometimes grow to five or six inches, are venomous. One good swipe from those nails and you're a gonner. Like bein' bit by a hundred rattlers, only more painful."

Listening to the story our three heroes weren't feeling very heroic. They were wondering if this whole thing was such a good idea after all.

"Maybe we should reconsider what we're doing here," said Ernie. "I mean learning to fly would be pretty cool but I'm pretty sure it's not worth meeting up with those dudes. We wouldn't stand a chance."

"Well I said it wouldn't be easy," said Calliope Rose. "But it ain't impossible. Stokes pretty much has 'em under control. Let me tell you a story. Seems that some time ago there was this dude named Rahm. Lived east of here. And by east I don't mean Chicago or New York. I mean way east, like India. Rahm was a good-lookin' kid and his daddy was some kind of high-falutin' big shot. A king or some such thing. But one day young Rahm gets to fussin' with his mama bout one thing or another and before you know it she up and throwed him outta the house. Can you imagine? Her own son.

"So Rahm takes his young wife, pretty little thing named Sita, and leaves the kingdom to live in the forest. Things were goin' along pretty good until one day Rahm comes home to find Sita gone. He looked everywhere but she was just nowhere to be found. Needless to say, he was heart broken. So he set out to try to find her. He traveled through the forest for several days until he came upon a band of monkeys.

"The Monkey King, can't remember his name now, told Rahm that Sita had been kidnapped by Rakshasas. Now Rahm was a pretty mellow dude, but I don't mind tellin' ya' this really ticked him off. He was madder'n a Hoot Owl at high noon. He vowed to track down those Rakshasas and save Sita. And that's exactly what he done.

"As I said before, them Rakshasas are real powerful-like, but Rahm had a couple of tricks up his sleeve too. Years before he had studied with some ol' cowboy named Vashti and he'd learned a thing or two 'bout fightin' hisself.

"So when he finally found em' he opened up a can of whup ass on those Rakshasas the likes you never seen.

Excuse my language, Hoggy, but that's what he done. Put a hurtin' on 'em somethin' fierce.

"A deadly battle took place and when it was over the forest was littered with dead Rakshasas. Rahm sent the survivors packin'. Told 'em ya'll don't come down through here no more. Or somethin' like that.

"A long time after that they showed up here in Big Sur causin' all kinds of mischief. Course it wasn't called Big Sur back then. Wasn't even a town yet, just a few settlers from the East. But after a while people were so scared they wouldn't even come out of their cabins.

"Then one day Stokes shows up. By this time Big Sur had become a town. Not a big one, mind you, but a town just the same. And like I said, Stokes shows up. Right here at the Inn. Stayed a few days then took off into the forest. Said he had some unfinished business to tend to.

"Now I don't know what happened out there in the forest. I wasn't here at the time. All I know is everyone said those Rakshasas stopped comin' round. Rumor has it there was a great battle and most of the Rakshasas were killed. A few escaped and left the forest to make their way in the outside world. Some of 'em went into the oil business or ended up workin' on Wall Street but most of the survivors went into politics and at least two became U.S. Presidents. Not many people know that but it's a fact just the same. There were some, including their leader, dude named Ravana, who weren't killed and also didn't escape. Stokes rounded 'em up and banished 'em to a part of the forest where they couldn't escape. He threw down some good ol' fashioned Cajun JuJu on 'em.

"Ju Ju?" said Hoggy.

"Yeah, like a Voodoo spell or somethin'. Don't rightly know exactly how it works, but he's got 'em locked up tight in a sort of forest prison. And they ain't getting out anytime soon either. The only way they can escape is to kill someone who accidentally wanders into their territory. But that ain't gonna happen cause everyone knows not to go anywhere near there. Might not even be any of 'em left by this time. Stokes cleared all the animals out fore he locked 'em up so there's nothing for 'em to eat. Knowin' them though they probably started eatin' each other."

"So Stokes is really Rahm?" said Hoggy.

"Not likely. Rahm woulda been too old by then. My guess is he taught Stokes a few things and Stokes just sorta took over the business of fightin' Rakshasas.

"What I do know is we haven't really had much trouble since Stokes showed up. But Stokes rarely comes to town and when he does, he don't say much. He always stays here at the Inn though. Fact is we even have a cabin named after him. Stokes' Room we call it. Now I ain't got no fancy book learnin' or nothin' like that. Not like Froggy here. But I know a thing or two about the forest and I know how to find the Path that'll take ya'll to Stokes' cabin.

"Like I said, it ain't gonna be easy but if you stay on the Path you'll be okay."

"What's the Path?" said Froggy.

"That's what I'm gonna show you."

Calliope Rose looked around the table, first at Ernie, then Hoggy, then Froggy.

"Well, what's it gonna be? You wanna find Stokes or what?"

No one said a word as they pondered the question. They were all looking down at the table, unable to look at each other. Finally Froggy broke the silence.

"I think we should go."

"Me too," said Hoggy. "Let's do it."

Ernie continued looking down. He really wanted to go, but he really, really wasn't looking forward to an encounter with a Rakshasa.

I could just stay here at the Inn, he thought. Let Froggy and Hoggy try to find Stokes. But what if they found him and learned how to fly? I would still be the only Woodpecker on the planet that couldn't fly. What to do? What to do?

Finally he looked up, glanced around the table and said, "I'm in."

"All right," said Hoggy. "I don't think I could have gone without you, Ernie. It just wouldn't be the same."

Froggy, for his part, never had any doubts about Ernie's decision. He knew him well enough to know that he would never let a girl show more bravery than him.

"Hold on a second." said Froggy, looking at Calliope Rose. "We have another slight problem."

"Yeah," said Ernie, remembering the stalker. "Someone's following us."

"Swami said something bout a fella might be hangin' round stirrin' up mischief. I wouldn't worry too much about him though. When you get on the Path you'll be okay. No one's ever been hurt once they're on the Path. It's a known fact. And just to make sure he don't bother us none between here and the Path I'm bringin' along a friend."

"Well I hope he's a big friend." said Hoggy. "This guy's scary."

"Not a he," said Calliope Rose as she walked to the kitchen, reached behind the door and pulled out a 12 gauge shotgun. "This here's Susan B."

"Jeeze," said Ernie. "You know how to use that thing?"

"Ain't been fired in years, but I keep her oiled up and you could bet your boots, if you had any, that I know how to use her. Ain't nobody messes with Susan B."

It had taken three AAA road side assistance tow trucks to wench the Hummer from the ditch but its armour plating had proved indestructible and it was now parked on the Coast Highway a hundred yards south of the Inn. The six panel Bose was receiving a clear signal and Reacher was able to listen to their conversation as if he were in the room with them. The Nikon Viper was locked in on the dining room window affording him a close up view of Calliope Rose.

So the old gal has a weapon, he thought. And she looks just mean enough to use it. He would have to be careful with that one. Calista was lightning fast but the blade had not yet been designed that was faster than the blast from a 12 gauge. He would wait until she left them alone on this so-called Path. Then they would see what could and could not be done. They would see what Calista was capable of. Despite all the set backs this was going to be as easy as he first thought.

CHAPTER 10

The next morning, before they set out on their journey, Calliope Rose gave each of them a thermos.

"What's this?" said Froggy.

"Iskiate," said Calliope Rose.

"Iskiate?" said Ernie. "I know about that."

"Ya'll should," said Calliope Rose. "Ximena fed it to you when you were hurt and she was nursin' you back to health. It's the secret super food of your old nemesis the Tarahumara Indians. They've been known to run through the mountains for days, sometimes for hundreds of miles, with nothin' to eat or drink but Iskiate. It'll keep ya' goin' for a few days as long as you ration it. Don't take much to give you the energy you need for a long hike. But just to make sure, I've got an extra supply for you right here. Hoggy can carry it."

She then gave Hoggy a small backpack and helped her put it on.

"So are you ready?" she said.

"Let's do it," said Hoggy.

Behind his sunglasses Ernie was rolling his eyes again, thinking she was starting to sound like a Nike commercial. But he didn't say anything.

So they left the Inn and headed into the forest, Calliope Rose leading the way. Summer was getting tired now but there were still some beautiful days left and this was one of them. A few puffs of white clouds stood out against a brilliant blue Big Sur sky.

In this part of the forest the trees were so far apart that there really was no Path. But as they continued deeper into the forest the trees grew closer together and the canopy cast by the ancient trees began to fill the sky. After about an hour they reached a river with a narrow bridge and Calliope Rose stopped.

"There it is," she said.

They looked around but didn't see anything resembling a Path.

"Where?" asked Froggy.

"Ya'll can't see it from here, but it's just the other side. Can't miss it. Well kids, this is where we part company. But I was wonderin', Ernie, would you mind if I drove Louise while you're gone? I'll take real good care of her."

"Uh, I don't know about that," he said.

"Come on Ernie," said Hoggy. "Once we like learn to fly you won't even need Louise."

Which wasn't true. Ernie could learn to fly to the moon and he still wouldn't give up Louise.

Finally he said, "Well, okay, but be careful. No one's ever driven her 'cept me and Froggy."

"No worries," she said. "She's in good hands."

But as she looked at Ernie, she could tell that he still didn't feel comfortable. And it had nothing to do with Louise.

"Don't worry," she said. "You guys'll be all right. Just remember to stay on the Path. No matter what happens, do not leave the Path. And remember, if there ain't no birds around that's not a good sign. Always listen for birds. But the main thing is: STAY ON THE PATH. Period. No matter what happens, never, ever leave the Path."

And with that she turned and started her hike back to the Inn. But she stopped, turned back to face them and said,

"Oh, one last thing. Be on the look out for Velociraptors."

“Velociraptors?” they cried in unison.

“Ha. Just kidding,” she said as she skipped off through the forest laughing and singing something about sideburns and staying alive.

“What a kidder she is,” said Froggy. But Ernie was not amused.

“Not funny, Froggy. Not funny at all.”

“Come on Ernie, lighten up,” said Hoggy. “This is gonna be like so much fun.”

Little did she know.

CHAPTER 11

They crossed the bridge and, sure enough, there was the Path, wide and smooth and meandering off through the forest.

They hadn't eaten since breakfast so they each had a big gulp of Iskiate and started off down the Path. As they walked along they could hear songbirds everywhere. A good sign when you're on the lookout for Rakshasas. They even heard the rat-a-tat-tat of a woodpecker.

"Hear that?" said Hoggy. "There's even woodpeckers here, Ernie. That's like such a good sign. You should feel right at home."

"Yeah, but they're not Imperial Woodpeckers. Probably some common variety." Ernie's pride was showing.

As they continued on, they were again taken by the magic that is Big Sur. The ancient redwoods with shaggy moss growing on their north side, the pine trees, not as tall, but majestic in their own right. There were California

Lace Ferns and flowers everywhere: phantom orchids, blue blossoms, Indian paint brush, dandelions, and crimson columbine. And, of course, the songbirds: Yellow bellied fly catchers, doves, larks, swallows, waxwings and warblers, sparrows, grosbeaks and finches. Overhead, soaring on the thermals, were vultures, condors, and hawks. And although they didn't see him, they could hear the Great Horned Owl.

So far the Path had followed the river and as the sun started to hang low in the sky, they decided to make camp until morning. They didn't have sleeping bags but Calliope Rose had assured them that a warm blanket was all that was needed.

They found a patch of level ground between two pine trees, which stood between the every present redwoods.

By this time the sun had found another home and darkness was all around. As they spread their blankets and looked up they could see the redwoods stretching out to touch the low hanging stars and moonlight licked the branches on its journey through the leaves to the forest floor.

They awoke the next morning eager to continue their journey. After a quick breakfast of Iskiate they set out following the Path that now led away from the river. It was another gorgeous day. The sun was shining bright, the songbirds were about, and a gentle breeze ruffled the red, purple, yellow, blue and pink flowers. It was a cascade of colors, a concert for the eyes.

As the sun grew brighter overhead, they decided to look for a nice spot for an Iskiate lunch. Close behind them

Reacher decided it was time to make his move. He was just about to leap from behind a tree when Ernie stopped.

"Hold on a sec guys, I have to pee."

"Okay," said Froggy. "We'll just go on up ahead and give you some privacy."

"No problem, dude. I'll just step behind this tree."

As Ernie turned toward the tree Hoggy cried out, "No, Ernie, don't." But it was too late. Ernie had taken one step off the Path. As his foot hit the ground, with just that one step off the Path, he was hit with a blast of cold, dry air. It was as if a hole had been torn through his world and he was thrust into another dimension.

The sun disappeared. It was suddenly dark. Not dark as night, more like a cold, cloudy day with smoke-like mist everywhere.

Uh oh, he thought. He turned around to step back on the Path but the Path wasn't there. No Froggy. No Hoggy. Only darkness. He could hear Froggy and Hoggy calling to him but their voices were distant, like in a dream.

"Come back, Ernie." That was Froggy.

"I can't see you," cried Ernie.

Both Hoggy and Froggy could see him, as he was just a few feet away. And they could hear him, too. But Ernie couldn't see the Path, couldn't see them, couldn't see the trees, and worst of all, didn't hear a single bird. Only silence.

He sensed something behind him and quickly turned around again. At first he saw only their outline, ghost like. They were slowly moving toward him and as they got closer their bodies came into focus. Huge bodies. Over twelve feet tall with eyes glowing a hideous red and yellow. They were horrible to look at with blood dripping from their saber-like teeth and long nails and an odor foul as a sewer. One of them carried a frog under one arm and a pig under the other.

"We already killed your friends, Woodpecker. And you're next."

"No," cried Ernie. "My friends are behind me."

The beast let out a roar of laughter.

"Ha. So you think. When you stepped off the Path you brought them with you. And now they're dead. Because you were too stupid to stay on the Path."

And with that he took a bite out of the pig, bit the head off of the frog, swallowed them both and let out a loud belch, his breath fouling the already putrid air.

"NO!" cried Ernie. "That can't be."

Ernie was beside himself with grief. His head pounded like thunder and blood boiled and screamed in his ears. His heart was being crushed in a vise that plunged fathom after fathom into a sea of darkness and despair. Because of him Froggy and Hoggy were dead. Tears welled up in his little woodpecker eyes and he cried like he'd never cried before.

Then he sensed something to his right and glanced over to see Reacher who, in an effort to go undetected, had ducked behind a tree and stepped off The Path at the exact same moment Ernie had. There was panic in his eyes and as the Rakshasa came closer he put his hand on Calista, preparing for the attack. A quick glance from the Rakshasa melted the blade, welding it to the bounty hunter's hand, his flesh dripping to the ground like molten lava flowing from a volcano. He slumped to the ground, his body a smoldering mass of unrecognizable flesh.

Then Ernie heard the voice again.

"Ernie, come back." It was Hoggy. But she sounded so far away.

"Froggy, why doesn't he come back?" she said.

"He can't see us. And he can barely hear us. He thinks we're far away."

So even though Ernie was just a few feet away, Froggy screamed as loud as he could.

"Just take two steps, Ernie. Go to the sound of my voice. We're right here."

Ernie took one step forward. Nothing. He was still in the dark. He glanced over his shoulder and saw the Rakshasa getting closer. He could almost feel his rotting breath. But he couldn't move. He was frozen in place. He couldn't move a single muscle in his feathered body. The Rakshasa was close now and reached out his terrible hand to whisk Ernie away.

At the same time, with both feet planted firmly on the Path and Hoggy holding him from behind, Froggy reached out, grabbed Ernie by the wing and, with a mighty tug, jerked him back onto the Path. He pulled so hard they all tumbled backwards and fell in a heap with a thump, thump, thump, thump. Ernie had bounced once.

As they got to their feet Hoggy was about to grab Ernie when Froggy stopped her.

"Wait a minute, Hoggy," he said.

And turning to Ernie, "Ernie, what's my name?"

Ernie looked puzzled.

"Your name?"

"My name."

"Your name's Froggy. That's a dumb question."

Ernie thought about this for a moment.

"Oh, I get it. You're just testing me to make sure it's really me. Like maybe the Rakshasas took over my body? Well, it's me, dude. Your old pal."

When Froggy didn't respond Ernie stared at the ground.

They don't believe me, he thought. They really don't believe it's me.

"Look Froggy..." he started to say. But Froggy cut him off.

"If we were back at Swami's Beach, what would we be doing?"

Ernie's eyes, which you could now plainly see since he had lost his sunglasses, a souvenir for the Rakshasas, lit up.

"Dude, you know what we'd be doing. We'd be sitting on our boards outside the surf line, waitin' for Big Rhino to roll in from Mexico. And when it arrived we'd be walkin' the nose, hangin' ten and shootin' the curl. We'd shred that sucker all the way to the beach. Then at the last second we'd kick out, paddle back out and do it all over again."

Hoggy, who was now huddled behind Froggy, peered out from her hiding place and looked up at him.

"I have like no idea what he just said, but does that mean it's him?"

Froggy broke out in a big frog grin.

"Sure does, Hoggy. That's our boy. No doubt about it. No Rakshasa would ever know any of that."

"Oh, Ernie, it's you," she said as she jumped forward, grabbed him by the wings, started doing a little dance and singing something about fishes. Then she hugged him, danced around some more, and hugged him again.

Then it was Froggy's turn. He wrapped his long arms around them both in a group hug.

"Nice to have you back, my brother."

"Dude, you have no idea. Calliope Rose was right. Never, ever step off the Path. It's way whack in there. Talk about ridin' the dragon's back. Dudes aren't messin' around, man. They're full-on serious bad news. Took over my mind and I couldn't move. Made me think you guys were dead. They're flat-out, pure grade A evil. They throw down a mojo and you're paralyzed.

Ernie went on like this for several seconds until, finally, Froggy interrupted him.

"Okay, Ernie. We get it."

"Sorry, dude, but until you see it with your own eyes you have no idea. But one good thing—we don't have worry about that stalker guy any more. The Rakshasas took care of him. Fried him like bacon in a pan."

"He was in there with you?" said Hoggy. "How did he get in there?"

"Probably stepped off the Path when Ernie did," said Froggy.

"Well, that's a relief," said Hoggy. "One less thing to worry about."

Froggy remembered what Calliope Rose had said about the only way the Rakshasas could escape. Not wanting to alarm his friends, he didn't say anything. But he could hear her voice loud and clear: *Those dudes are nothin' to mess around with. Just stay on the Path. No one's ever been hurt once they're on the Path. It's a known fact.* They would have to trust the Innkeeper on this one.

Then Hoggy started her little dance again, singing to no one in particular about some kind of a celebration with fishes. Strange little pig, thought Ernie.

Meanwhile, high above them, a lone Eagle rode the thermals looking down with great interest at a pig, a frog, and a woodpecker.

CHAPTER 12

Ernie was wiped out from his little encounter with the Rakshasas and said he needed a nap before he could go on. He took a swig of Iskiate, spread his blanket out right in the middle of the Path (no use taking any chances) and laid down. But within twenty minutes the Iskiate worked its magic. He stood up completely rejuvenated and declared himself "ready to roll."

And roll they did. They were well into their second day on the Path and sensed they might be getting closer to their goal. They started up the Path with a renewed sense of optimism.

Behind them, after 150 years of incarceration, the great Ravana, King of the Rakshasas, stepped from his forest prison onto the Path in the form of the bounty hunter known as Reacher. His trusted lieutenants, all twenty of them, stepped onto the Path behind him.

"Let's get em'," said one. "I'm hungry."

"NO!" commanded Ravana. It wasn't a request. "It's not them we want. Stokes is expecting them and if they don't show up he'll know we escaped. We can ill afford another battle with Stokes. Have you forgotten our last encounter? Those three won't be here forever and when they leave we'll get our revenge by taking Stokes' wife. I know a place twenty miles up river where we can camp until the time is right. There's plenty of game to feed us and it's far enough away that Stokes won't know we're here. The animals talk to him so we have to keep our distance for now. I'll post sentries near the cabin. They'll stay out of sight and report back to me. The pig thinks she's going to learn how to fly. How stupid can she be? Pigs can't fly. When they finally learn the folly of this they'll leave and we'll take the wife."

There was some grumbling among the ranks but no one dared question the great Rakshasa's authority.

About two hours later Froggy, who was leading the way, stopped.

"I don't know if you guys noticed, but we have company."

Hoggy and Ernie froze in their tracks, looking first this way, then that way. They turned in a circle, horrified that they might be looking into the eyes of a dreaded Rakshasa.

Seeing nothing but trees, flowers and a few butterflies, Ernie spoke first. "If this is some kind of a joke, Froggy, it's not funny at all."

"No joke. Look up."

They looked up but all they saw was a lone bird, so high up as to not be threatening.

"All I see is a bird," said Hoggy.

"Not just any bird," said Froggy. "That's a Bald Eagle. And what you don't see are hawks, turkey vultures or condors. Probably because he chased them all away. There's only room for one king of the skies, and he's it."

"But he's so far away," said Hoggy. "How can you tell it's an eagle?"

"He's up pretty high. I'd say about a mile. But the fact that we can plainly see him tells me it's an eagle. Only an eagle would look that big from so far away. Of course the Andean Condor is just as big, maybe bigger, but they live down south. Nope, that's definitely a Bald Eagle. They can have a wing span of eight feet, almost as wide as the Path."

Hoggy and Ernie looked down trying to imagine a bird whose wings were large enough to cover the Path.

Froggy continued. "They can cruise at about 10,000 feet, almost two miles. At 5,000 feet, which is about where this guy is, they can spot a rabbit moving through the forest. I thought I saw an eagle's nest a while back but it was way too small. Probably a condor or hawk's nest. An eagle's nest can be more than eight feet wide and thirteen feet deep. They can weigh as much as 2000 pounds, which, by the way, is one ton! But the reason I know for sure it wasn't an eagle's nest is that an eagle would never have let us get that close. They attack anything that threatens the nest. And I don't mean to scare you, Hoggy, but this guy is strong enough to pluck you right out of your shoes. If you were wearing any, that is. So we would be wise to keep an eye on him because you can bet Louise's pink slip he's watching us. He's been circling for about an hour and he's getting closer. He started out much higher up but he loses altitude with every circle."

"If it's not one thing it's another," said Ernie. "First Rakshasas and now this. And if he gets any closer there's no place to hide without leaving the Path."

"As if," said Hoggy. "That is so not going to happen. I'll take my chances with an eagle over a Rakshasa any day."

"Your chances would be about the same with both," said Froggy. "But let's not fret too much now. Just keep an eye on him."

Before starting out again they all looked to the sky, and sure enough, there he was. But closer now.

It was starting to get dark when they came to a dried out riverbed. The Path seemed to end. It didn't go on to the left or to the right.

"What now?" said Hoggy.

They looked around until Froggy spoke first.

"Unless the Path goes straight up the river bed, which isn't likely, I'd say it continues on the other side."

They crossed the river bed only to find that there was no Path there either. They froze.

"We're off the Path," cried Hoggy.

"I don't think so," said Ernie. "Believe me, if we were off the Path we'd know it. Look. There are still trees and flowers. But best of all, listen. Hear the birds?"

"So," said Hoggy, "we're not off the Path, but we're not exactly on it either. Or maybe we are and just don't know it. I'm like so confused."

"Let's just keep going in a straight line from where the Path ended on the other side," said Froggy. "If we don't find anything we can always double back."

So keeping in mind where the Path had ended, they set off through the forest.

After about an hour darkness unpacked its bags and decided to settle in for the night. But there was a three-quarter moon so there was still enough light to keep going. But after awhile they couldn't tell if they were still moving in a direct line from where the Path had ended.

Then, out of nowhere, a gang of rogue thunderclouds came rolling in from the north, looking for trouble. And they weren't alone. Intent on hijacking the sky, they brought their old friend lightning. Completely outnumbered, the moon didn't stand a chance. Together they cracked open the sky and short-circuited the moon, which flickered twice and then went out. The clouds were in charge now and any movement at all was like wading through a tsunami of ink.

With no chance of going on, they decided to camp right where they were. No one said anything, but it was becoming more and more obvious: THEY WERE LOST.

CHAPTER 13

Midnight. Froggy and Ernie had quickly slipped into a dreamless sleep, but Hoggy was wide-awake and sat motionless, staring into the darkness. If she had had a hand, which she didn't, she would not have been able to see it right in front of her face.

She sat that way for three full hours, barely blinking. Then her eyes started playing tricks on her. She thought she saw a tiny burst of light that shone for less than a second and then disappeared. Then another. And another. She blinked a few times thinking she was just tired. But the little lights kept popping up. It was making her dizzy and her stomach was feeling queasy.

"Guys," she said, "I don't feel so good."

"What is it, Hoggy?" said Froggy.

"I don't know. I'm like so dizzy. I don't feel good at all."

"Just go back to sleep, Hoggy. You'll feel better in the morning."

But she couldn't go back to sleep and the longer she stared into the darkness the more the little lights kept popping up all around. Finally she could take it no longer.

"Guys, I'm not kidding. I really don't feel so hot. Wake up, Froggy."

Froggy and Ernie opened their eyes, sat up and looked around.

"Ha," said Froggy. "It's only fireflies."

"Go back to sleep," said Ernie.

But before anyone could go back to sleep, the fireflies seemed to multiply. Ten turned into fifty. Then a hundred. Then a thousand. Then thousands, all flying around blinking their lights like tiny beacons in the night. Within a few seconds there were millions of tiny lights flashing on and off, lighting up the forest floor like a full moon on the 4th of July.

Then, as if on cue, the cloud of light moved several yards away, hovered, and then moved back, surrounding them again in a pure white light. When they moved away a second time, Hoggy said, "I think they want us to follow them."

"I think you're right," said Froggy.

So they quickly gathered their blankets and hurried after them.

The cloud of fireflies waited until they were close, and then began making their way through the forest, moving slowly enough to be followed. There were so many of them by now that they cast a light so bright it was like walking in the midday sun.

It seemed like they were walking in a circle and, sure enough, after about two miles they found themselves back at the dried out river bed and the Path that had ended on the other side.

As they approached the river bed, the fireflies turned left and started following the riverbed until again, as if connected by some cosmic radar, the giant cloud dispersed and formed a long line leading back into the forest, hovering about six feet off the ground.

Ernie was the first to notice.

"Look," he said.

Froggy and Hoggy stopped to see Ernie staring at the ground. It was like a miracle.

"The Path!" cried Hoggy. "We're back on the Path!"

The fireflies had led them back to the Path. Then, as quickly as they had appeared, the fireflies were gone. The lights went out and they were again surrounded by darkness.

There was no use trying to go on so they unrolled their blankets again and quickly slipped into the sleep of the innocent.

Hoggy, as usual, dreamed of pigs flying.

CHAPTER 14

They were so tired from their midnight trek through the forest that they slept well past sunrise. Hoggy was the first to wake. The clouds were off bothering someone else, and as she opened her eyes she found herself looking up at a bright blue Big Sur sky. She rolled over and propped herself up to see exactly where they were. But she never got a chance to look around because she found herself looking into the bright yellow eyes of the biggest bird she had ever seen. He was dark brown, almost black, with a white head and tail. He stood nearly three feet tall, had a large yellow hooked beak, and yellow feet that ended in huge powerful looking talons.

An eagle, she thought, probably the one that's been following us.

She tried to call out to Froggy, but couldn't find her voice. Behind her Froggy and Ernie began to stir.

"Don't move, Hoggy." It was Froggy.

Well that wasn't going to be a problem since, like Ernie with the Rakshasas, she too was paralyzed with fear. She would have run away if she could but she could only sit motionless, staring into those cold yellow eyes.

They sat staring at the great bird, not knowing what to do. Ernie glanced at Froggy, then back at the eagle.

Think of a plan, Froggy, he thought. Come on, dude, think of a plan.

"What's the matter?" said the eagle. "You don't recognize an old friend?"

Where have I heard that voice? thought Hoggy. But Froggy and Ernie recognized it immediately.

"Swami!" they cried in unison. They almost tripped over each other scrambling to hug their old friend.

"Boy am I glad to see you," said Ernie.

"Swami?" said Hoggy. She was so relieved she thought she might pass out. And that's exactly what she did. She fell over backwards with her little pig legs, all four of them, pointed to the sky.

She was only out for a couple of minutes, and when she came back to the world she found herself being attended to by Swami, now looking like his old familiar surfer self, while Froggy and Ernie looked on.

"Didn't mean to scare you little one," he said. "I thought for sure you saw me following you yesterday."

"Swam' dude," said Ernie. "We saw you but we thought you were just some hungry eagle stalking us for lunch."

"My bad," said Swami.

"But why the eagle costume?" said Froggy.

"Well I didn't know exactly where you were and it's easier for an eagle to cruise through the forest than a surfer. I came to see if you were making any progress, but as it turns out you didn't need my help after all. You found it!"

"Found what?" said Hoggy.

"Stokes' cabin, of course."

They looked around and saw nothing but forest.

"Stokes' cabin?" said Froggy.

"Yep. The Path ends about fifty yards from here. Right around that bend up to the right. It ends at Stokes' cabin."

"We're here?" cried Hoggy. "You mean we're here? We finally made it?"

"You sure did, Hoggy. But, listen, I gotta go now. Got a date with some big waves." He winked at Froggy and Ernie.

"Give my regards to Stokes. And sorry again for the fright. Oh, by the way, Ernie, here, you might need these." He pulled out a brand new pair of sunglasses and handed them to Ernie.

"Wow," said Ernie, "Oakleys. How cool. Thanks, dude."

"Only the best for my surfing bud," said Swami.

And with that he returned to his eagle form, took off down the dried-out river bed, banked left and went soaring through the forest heading south in search of Big Rhino.

As Froggy and Ernie watched the great bird swooping along the Path, Hoggy broke into the same dance she had performed with Ernie earlier. She was humming a tune and crying, "We made it, we made it." Strange little pig, thought Ernie.

When Hoggy had finished her dance they quickly snatched up their blankets and started up the Path at a very fast pace. As they neared the bend in the Path they slowed to a walk, almost tiptoeing, curious to see what they might find.

PART FOUR
STOKES

CHAPTER 15

They stood huddled behind a Monterey Pine, peering out to see what they could see. The Path ended abruptly at two stately redwoods about fifty feet apart, standing sentinel before a large flat area about the size of a football field.

And there, just beyond, was the cabin. Stokes' cabin. Even though they knew they had been looking for a cabin, they expected something a bit more elegant. But it was, indeed, just a cabin. Large, to be sure, but a cabin just the same.

It looked similar to the Inn with two exceptions. It was surrounded by the most beautiful garden they had ever seen and the roof was completely covered with solar panels.

Flowers sprang from the rich soil for a hundred feet on each side of the cabin, interrupted only by tiny paths weaving their way through the forest of color.

Some flowers were tall, nearly six feet, while others hugged the ground. Surrounding the garden, snuggled up against the redwoods were giant California ferns, some completely unfurled, ten feet across and eight feet tall. Some were still in the fiddlehead stage, ripe, they would later find out, for cooking.

They couldn't see it from where they were standing, but behind the cabin and beyond the flowerbeds was a vegetable garden planted with every imaginable vegetable.

There was arugula, bok choy, broccoli rabe, cabbage and celery, carrots, Chinese cabbage, mizuna greens, mustard greens, radicchio and spinach. There was Swiss chard, pumpkin, sweet pepper, squash, corn, tomatoes, broccoli, cauliflower and zucchini. And there were beans everywhere: black eyed peas, chickpeas, green beans, lentils and okra. There was asparagus, celery and wild leek. There were bamboo shoots, beet root and burdock, radishes, sweet potato and turnips. And Ernie's favorite, globe artichokes, with flowers that looked like gargantuan purple sea anemones.

Beyond the vegetable garden was a forest of fruit trees. There was apricot, apple, avocado and almond. There was cherry, cashew, jackfruit and olive. There were peaches, plums, persimmons and pears. There were saffron robed oranges and tangerines, all bowing low, offering their wares, ripe for the picking.

On the east side of the cabin, near the front door and surrounded by flowers, were four heavy redwood beams coming out of the ground to support a round glass canopy overhead. Suspended by four heavy bamboo chains from the middle of the canopy was a circular bed ten feet across. It seemed to be floating in mid-air.

Next to the front door was a young woman. Well, maybe not so young, as there were a few streaks of gray in her dark brown shoulder length hair. Not so young, but not old either. A real babe thought Ernie. But he didn't say anything.

She was kneeling in the dirt, tending to the flowers, and when she saw them approaching she stood up to greet them. She was tall, almost as tall as Swami, with long tan arms and legs. She was barefoot and wearing cut-off jeans and a faded blue work shirt.

As she got nearer they could see her clear brown eyes with flecks of green and gold.

"You finally made it," she said as she hugged them each in turn. It was as if they were lifelong friends.

"Stokes told me not to worry, but you never can tell what might happen out in the forest. My name is Vidya and you must be Froggy, Hoggy and Ernie."

They were so overwhelmed by the beauty of the garden and by Vidya's warm reception that they hardly knew what to say. It was as if they had entered another world, free of stalkers, Rakshasas and worry and stress.

"You must come inside," said Vidya. "I've prepared a nice soup for you. After a few days of Iskiate you must be ready for some real food."

"Amen to that," said Ernie.

"That would be real nice, Ms. Vidya," said Froggy.

"Please, Froggy, just Vidya. No need for formalities out here," she said.

They followed her to the front door and when they entered the cabin they got another surprise.

"Go ahead and look around," she said. "Make yourself at home. I'll just be a minute."

As they looked around they could see that there were no walls partitioning off separate rooms. It was one big room like you might find in an artist's loft in the city.

The entire east side of the cabin was two large picture windows, one on each side of the door. To the left was a thoroughly modern kitchen except there was one thing missing. There was no refrigerator. But everything else was right up to date. There was a stainless steel six-burner stove with convection oven for baking and a large triple stainless steel sink for washing fruits and vegetables and cleaning dishes. In the middle of the kitchen stood a large rectangular island made of bamboo with copper pots of all kinds hanging from a canopy overhead. The cabin's ceiling was almost twenty feet high and in one corner was another "floating bed."

Actually, there was one room partitioned off for privacy —the bathroom. But this was no ordinary bathroom. The floor, made of river stones, was heated. There was an open shower and a bathtub big enough for four. To one side was a steam room with glass walls and the walls to the outside were also made of glass, affording a view of the garden.

In the middle of the room was a large fireplace open on all four sides. The cabin floor was covered in carpets of all colors and instead of furniture there were pillows of all shapes and sizes strewn about the floor.

“Soup’s on,” said Vidya, so they made their way back to the kitchen and seated themselves at the island on tall stools, also made from bamboo.

Vidya ladled out a hearty soup and offered them good home baked bread, hard on the outside and pillowy soft on the inside.

“This is like totally the best soup ever,” said Hoggy. “What is it?”

“Ha,” said Vidya. “It’s called fas’oulada. But that’s just a fancy name for navy beans, carrots, celery and tomatoes. I added some fiddleheads from the ferns, too. It’s from Greece. Stokes and I used to live there.”

“Well it certainly is delicious, wherever it’s from,” said Froggy.

As they ate their fill, Hoggy could no longer contain herself.

“Vidya, can I ask you a question?”

“Let me guess. You want to know where Stokes is.”

“How did you know?”

“A reasonable guess. I would venture to say you didn’t travel four hundred miles just to sample my soup. It may be pretty good but I don’t think anyone would travel all that way and risk an encounter with Rakshasas just to taste it. As for Stokes, he’s out in the forest doing who knows what. But he should be back shortly. He never misses his midday meal.”

CHAPTER 16

After lunch, Vidya suggested they enjoy the afternoon sun, so they adjourned to the garden. Froggy and Ernie were lounging on the "floating bed" and Vidya was showing Hoggy the garden. Girl talk. She was pointing out the various flowers and introducing her three cats, Willoughby, Mister and Oliver, when three dogs bounded out of the forest. Well, actually only two bounded. The third sort of hopped and skipped. The two bounders were large, shaggy, black haired and looked like small bears. The hopper and skipper was a small brown and white Corgi.

"Oh, look, Belles," said Vidya to one. "Look who's come to see you. It's Hoggy, Froggy and Ernie. How lucky you are to have so many visitors. What a lucky boy."

And to the other small bear she said, "Look who's come to see you, Gracie. What a lucky girl you are. Guys, I'd like you to meet Belles, short for Beelzebub, and Gracie. And this little one here is Louise. Yes, Ernie, another Louise. You should get on famously."

Belles and Gracie greeted the strangers with tails wagging and licks from their huge tongues, while Louise quietly ignored them. You've seen one visitor, you've seen them all was her motto.

"Well," said Vidya. "If the kids are back that means Stokes can't be far behind."

As soon as she said this, the air was filled with song:

"I'm tryin' to stay alive
and keep my sideburns, too.
Ask all the people,
it's getting hard to do.
You've got a choice by yourself to make
to keep a bad job or take a break
Try to live a song in silence
with no ideas of violence
I'm tryin' to stay alive
but how about you?
Better stop and think about it."

Ernie immediately recognized it as on old rock and roll song. He was thinking that couldn't possibly be Stokes.

Froggy hadn't given much thought as to what Stokes might possibly look like. But Hoggy and Ernie had definite ideas as to his appearance.

Hoggy was sure he would look like some kind of holy man in white robes and sandals, with long white hair and beard and maybe carrying a walking staff.

Ernie was sure he would look like a mountain man, tall and broad of shoulder with a shaggy black beard, and dressed in a flannel shirt with suspenders, jeans and sturdy work boots.

As Stokes strode from the forest they could see they were both wrong. Stokes was shirtless and, like Vidya, barefoot. He wore only a simple pair of light cotton pants. He had shoulder length light brown hair and was clean-shaven. His sleepy almond shaped eyes seemed to take in everything and nothing at all. They shone as if there was a light burning in his skull. His walk was more of an effortless glide, as if he occupied no space.

Stokes was of medium height, not quite as tall as Vidya, had long tan arms, and although slender, was broad in the chest and shoulders with a prominent collarbone.

Approaching, he extended his hand for all to shake, but when he got to Ernie he gave him a high five instead.

"Cool sunglasses," he said.

Then, looking at all three, "You finally made it. And I see you've met Vidya and the kids, so if you'll excuse me, I'm late for lunch. Smells like fas'oulada from here."

Then, winking at Ernie, "I'm hungrier than a woodpecker with a headache. Ha. I got that one from Calliope

Rose. She always did have a way with words." And with that he disappeared into the cabin.

"Man, that was one cool entrance," said Ernie.

But Hoggy, quick to judge someone by their appearance, wasn't impressed. She was thinking a man who supposedly knew so much should appear more dignified. But she had been wrong before, and boy was she wrong this time.

CHAPTER 17

After finishing his meal Stokes gathered everyone onto the "floating bed" outside in the garden.

"So," he said. "Swami tells me you're in the market for some flying lessons."

They all nodded in agreement.

"Well, it's no parlor trick, you know. It's not something you go around showing off. I will have to admit, though, it does come in handy from time to time. And learning it is easy. Once you know the trick. But like everything else, it takes practice. Most people won't take the time to practice. They're either too busy or they don't see immediate results. They get disappointed and before you know it, they've stopped altogether. But if you practice you'll get results."

"That's no problem," said Hoggy. "I'll like practice all day everyday if that's what it takes."

Stokes laughed. "That won't be necessary, Hoggy. A few minutes a couple of times a day is sufficient. But before we get into that let's perform a little experiment. I want you to close your eyes and just sit quietly for a couple of minutes."

They closed their eyes until Stokes said, "Okay, open your eyes and tell me what you were thinking."

"I was thinking about flying," said Hoggy.

"I was thinking about Vidya's soup," said Ernie.

"And I was thinking how lucky you are to live in such beautiful surroundings," added Froggy.

"Okay, good," said Stokes. "Now let's try it again, only this time I want you to think about nothing. No thoughts at all."

So they closed their eyes again and after a minute or two Stokes said, "Okay, how did it go? No thoughts, right?"

"It's impossible," said Froggy. "Unless you're asleep you can't stop thinking. And even then you sometimes dream. And that's thinking. It just can't be done."

"That's where you're wrong, Froggy. There's a place in the mind where there are no thoughts. And if you know how to get there all that mind chatter stops. That's what you have to learn before you learn the secret of flying."

"So it's like a meditation?" said Hoggy.

"You can call it anything you like, Hoggy. Naming it isn't important. What's important is learning it and then practicing everyday."

“Oh, good,” she said. “I want to call it meditation. It would be so totally awesome to be able to tell people I meditate.”

“Sounds too good to be true,” said Ernie. “I’ll bet it takes years and years to learn something like that. And we don’t have much time.”

“Actually it takes only a few minutes,” said Stokes. “And like I said, after that it’s just a matter of practice. And you may have more time than you think.”

“So when can we learn?” asked Froggy, always the practical one.

“How about right now,” said Stokes.

“You mean it?” said Hoggy. “Right this very minute? That would be like totally awesome.”

“Yes, Hoggy, I mean right this very minute. And once you’ve learned you might have a different concept of awesome.”

“Let’s do it,” she said.

Ernie was thinking there she goes again with the Nike commercial.

So one by one Stokes took them into the cabin and, seated on a comfortable pillow, whispered the instructions in their ear.

After receiving the instruction they were told to sit quietly for a few minutes and practice. So they did. When they were finished, Stokes gathered them outside again and asked them about their experience.

"Well I don't feel that much different," said Hoggy, rather disappointed. She had expected some kind of cosmic revelation. "I guess I feel like kind of calm. But that's about it."

"Me, too," said Ernie. "Not much at all."

"Well, I definitely feel calm," said Froggy. "But energized too. Like I just had a good night's sleep. Is that all there is to it?"

"It's as simple as that," said Stokes. "Now it's just a matter of practice. After awhile you'll have more energy than you ever dreamed possible. And you'll develop an inner calm like you can't believe."

Vidya, who had been watching from a distance, approached them and couldn't help notice a change. They may not have felt that much different, but she could see it in their eyes. They were more focused, and sparkled with an inner light. They were well on their way, she thought.

CHAPTER 18

As the days passed, they settled into a routine. They would practice their meditation for a few minutes morning and evening and in between they spent their time in any number of ways.

Ernie was fond of riding through the forest on the back of either Gracie or Belles, but not Louise. Louise was having nothing at all to do with that nonsense.

Froggy spent his time walking, or in his case hopping, through the forest with Stokes who would point out different plants that were good for eating, which were poisonous, and which were "good medicine."

There was foxglove, which looked like a tall cylinder, made up of purple, pink and white bells. That was good medicine for the heart. There was Queen of the Meadow, the root of which was good for a toothache and whose flowers made tasty jams and jellies.

There were so many that Froggy, who was pretty smart and a quick learner, could barely keep up. And Stokes knew them all. Hoggy would later learn from Vidya that neither she nor Stokes ever got sick, but Stokes knew them all anyway.

For her part Hoggy learned all about the garden. She learned the names of all the flowers and how and when to best plant and tend to the vegetables.

And she learned the reason there was no refrigerator. There was nothing to refrigerate! They ate everything fresh from the garden and never prepared more than they could eat each day. There were goats to provide fresh milk, but never more than was needed. And the goats, who would normally eat anything and everything, had been trained to eat any weeds that might pop up in the garden, leaving the flowers untouched.

One day while Hoggy was learning to milk the goats, Vidya stopped her and looked around as if to make sure no one was listening.

"Can you keep a secret, Hoggy?"

"Are you kidding? I'm like the best secret keeper ever."

Which wasn't true. There was nothing Hoggy liked more than a nice juicy piece of gossip. And she just couldn't help telling someone. But in her mind she wasn't really revealing the secret. She was only telling someone who wouldn't tell anyone else.

"What is it, Vidya? Tell me. Tell me."

"I've never told anyone this, but I think I can trust you."

"Yes, yes. What is it?"

"Well... Stokes isn't who he says he is. And neither am I."

"What do you mean? If he's not Stokes, who is he?"

"His real name is Rahm."

"Wait a minute," said Hoggy. "If Stokes is really Rahm, then you must be..."

"Sita. Yes, Hoggy, my given name is Sita."

Hoggy was speechless. She sat staring at Vidya, or Sita, or whatever her name was, with her mouth hanging open like some kind of half-wit.

"But that's impossible," she said. "If Stokes is Rahm and you're Sita, that would make you like a couple of hundred years old. No way."

"Try 9,000 years," said Sita.

"9,000?" cried Hoggy.

"Shh. Keep your voice down. Yes, 9,000. Rahm was born in 7,323 B.C. and I was born shortly after."

"Come on Vidya, I mean Sita. No one can live that long. This is like a joke, right?"

"No joke, Hoggy. Calliope Rose probably told you about me being kidnapped by the Rakshasas? Whew. That was a long time ago but believe me, it's something I'll never forget. But before that Rahm had studied with a friend of his dad's. Very wise man by the name of Vasistha. Calliope Rose met him once. She liked to call him Vashti. Anyway, Vasistha taught him a lot of cool stuff, including how to stop the ageing process. Well, not stop it exactly, but slow it down considerably. I don't know if you noticed but I do have a few gray hairs."

Hoggy, not famous for her sense of humor, said, "Why Vidya, you don't look a day over 5,000." They had a laugh.

"So Rahm taught me this little ageing trick and for almost 9,000 years we're been moving from one place to another. As our friends started to age, we didn't. In order to avoid suspicion, we moved every forty years or so. In 9,000 years we traveled all over India, Africa, most of Europe, South America, Australia, Canada and now finally here in the United States. First on the East Coast and then slowly we moved west.

"But I got tired of moving so we ended up here and took the names Stokes and Vidya. We've been in this forest since before the Civil War, long before it was called Big Sur.

"Only four people know our secret. Calliope Rose is one, and the original owner of the Inn, a gentleman that went by the name of Helmuth Deetjen, is another. And then, of course there's Swami. And even though Calliope Rose knows our secret, even she doesn't know how long we've been here.

"When we first got here we lived like nomads, roaming through the forest and never staying in one place. This was no big deal for Rahm. After all we'd been doing it for thousands of years. But I wanted a place to call home so Rahm enlisted the help of Helmuth and the two of them built this cabin for me. Over the years Stokes, usually with the help of Swami, who, by the way is a few thousand years old himself, have made improvements on the cabin. Like solar heating and a nice modern kitchen and bathroom!"

"Wow," said Hoggy. "Swami is really that old?"

"Yeah. I don't know exactly how old, but he's been around for awhile."

"How come he doesn't live here in the forest with you guys? You bein' old friends and all."

"That's simple. There's no surfing here. And Swami loves his surfing. Funny thing, though. People in Southern California don't think it odd that a Swami is also a surfer. And they don't seem to notice that he doesn't age. Must be something in the water."

"But you said there were four people who knew your secret. You only mentioned three."

"Oh, yeah. The fourth is an old friend of ours, Patanjali; he taught us how to fly in exchange for Stokes teaching him how not to age."

"Patanjali?" said Hoggy.

"Yes. But he changed his name too. Now he's called Fred."

"Fred? Fred what?"

"Just Fred. So that's my secret, Hoggy. Please keep it to yourself. Stokes would have a cow if he knew I told you."

"But what shall I call you, Sita or Vidya?"

"Just call me Vidya. And Rahm is still Stokes. Don't ever forget that."

For the first time in her life Hoggy thought she actually could keep a secret. It would be kind of fun knowing something that Froggy and Ernie didn't. That would be totally different for a change. And whom would she tell anyway? They were her only friends.

"So now that I've told you my secret," said Vidya, "you have to tell me yours."

"Mine? I don't have a secret. What do you mean?"

"I mean that little dance I see you doing. You know the one?"

"The Hukilau? You want to learn the Hukilau? For real?"

"I'd love to learn it, if it's not too hard. It looks complicated."

"No, it's not. I could like teach you so fast. It's easy."

Hoggy couldn't believe someone actually wanted to learn something from her. That had never happened before.

"Let's do it," said Vidya.

Stokes, Froggy, Ernie, Belles, Gracie and Louise had been in the forest. As they neared the cabin they could hear it:

"Oh we're going to a hukilau
a huki huki huki huki hukilau
Everybody loves the hukilau
where the laulau is the kaukau at the luau
We throw our nets into the sea
and all the amaama come a swimming to me
Oh, we're going to a hukilau
a huki huki huki hukilau.

And there, in the middle of the garden, hips and arms swaying back and forth, toes pointed first this way and then that, were Hoggy and Vidya. Singing and dancing the Hukilau.

They didn't see the guys approaching and were quite surprised and just a tiny bit embarrassed when they got a standing ovation.

"That's a pretty cool little dance you got going for you, Hoggy," said Stokes. "And I see you've got Vidya doing it too. What's it called?"

"It's the Hukilau," said Hoggy quite proudly. "It's from Hawaii. It's about a luau? You know, like a party? I like it cause they're singing about catching and eating fish instead of pigs!"

Finally Ernie said it out loud: "You are one strange little pig, Hoggy."

But he was smiling and she could tell he meant it in a good way.

Ravana had placed his spies about fifty yards from the cabin, one on each side. They worked in shifts and reported back to Ravana every two days. There was little for them to report but at least their grumbling had stopped. They had an entire forest from which to hunt game and were no longer hungry for the first time in years. They didn't really care if the stupid pig and her friends stayed in the forest forever. They didn't share Ravana's thirst for revenge and had little desire for another encounter with Stokes.

They had taken the shape of humans but the birds sensed their presence and began to leave the area surrounding the cabin. Their migration happened so slowly that no one seemed to notice their dwindling numbers. No one, that is, except Belles, Gracie and Louise. They became reluctant to leave the garden when Stokes went for a walk. They knew Stokes could take care of himself but Vidya was vulnerable. Their instinct was to protect her. They took turns staying awake at night and one of them was always by her side, usually Belles. There was something wrong but they didn't know what it was.

They debated whether or not to tell Stokes about their concerns but decided to just wait and watch. Maybe they were just being overly protective.

They should have followed their instincts because Ravana, unlike his lieutenants, was getting restless. He was starting to think maybe they should just kill the three visitors and take Vidya when Stokes was out for a walk. If he timed it just right they could be long gone before Stokes knew what had happened. It was risky business but he always knew there would be risk. Stokes had tracked him down before so he would have to be more careful this time. But the prize was worth the risk and the time was near.

CHAPTER 19

After awhile Hoggy began to get antsy. In fact they were all getting a bit fidgety. They were feeling pretty mellow and had a surprising new energy level, but there was still only one thing on their minds. When do we learn to fly? Stokes had told them to be patient, said he would tell them when the time was right, but Hoggy just couldn't take the suspense any longer.

One night during the evening meal she said, "Excuse me, Stokes, but when…"

"Tomorrow," he said.

"Tomorrow?"

"Tomorrow you learn to fly."

"But how did you know what I was… never mind. You mean it? Really?" Tomorrow's the day?"

"Tomorrow's the day," he said. "And if I were you I'd get a good night's sleep."

And with that he and Vidya left the cabin to take a moonlight walk.

The next day they had an early breakfast and gathered outside, eagerly waiting for Stokes to awaken. But Stokes was nowhere around. He had left very early with the dogs for a walk in the forest.

As the sun crawled higher in the sky they paced back and forth through the garden. They heard him before they saw him:

"I'm trying to stay alive
And keep my sideburns too."

He came strolling from the forest.

"Follow me," he said.

They followed him into the cabin and watched as he pulled back one of the carpets to reveal a trap door. He opened the door and started down the steep steps signaling them to follow.

They followed him to the bottom of the staircase, which opened onto a large room, a footprint of the entire cabin. As was the case upstairs, there were no interior walls. And no furniture either. The entire room, including the walls and ceiling were covered with foam mattresses.

"For your protection" said Stokes, pointing to the foam.

"When you first learn you may have trouble directing your flight. Better to land on or crash into foam than something less forgiving." They would soon learn first hand the wisdom in this.

They gathered around Stokes and, unlike their meditation instructions, which were given in private, they received their flying lesson in a group. The whole thing took less than five minutes.

"That's all there is?" said Froggy.

"That's it," said Stokes. "It's the same concept as your meditation. Just think the words. But don't try to concentrate and don't expect anything. Let it happen. You'll take off before you know it. They'll be short flights at first, so don't mind where you end up. You can learn to direct it later. Well, you're on your own. Go for it."

They each settled in corners of the room, closed their eyes, and began thinking the secret words. After about ten minutes they heard Stokes ringing a tiny bell.

"Okay, time's up," he said.

"Already?" said Hoggy. "But nothing happened."

"Oh, something happened all right," said Stokes. "You just didn't notice it. From now on I want you to practice for ten minutes twice a day after your meditation. After some time we can try fifteen or twenty minutes. But for now just ten minutes."

Hoggy was not happy about this at all. She wanted to fly and she wanted to fly right now.

"Whatever," she said.

For the next few days they practiced twice a day but didn't see any results at all. Froggy and Ernie had both felt a little trembling in their body but certainly no one was flying.

On the fifth day Hoggy heard a commotion and opened her eyes to find Froggy about ten feet from where he usually sat and Ernie was… it couldn't be! Ernie was suspended in mid-air! But only for a few seconds. As she watched in disbelief, Ernie floated back to the floor and landed softly right where he had started.

Then Froggy was flying through the air again. Until he hit the wall. He fell to the floor and he and Ernie rolled around laughing.

"Too cool," said Ernie. "Did you see that, dude? I must have been in the air for like twenty seconds. And Froggy, you were awesome, man. Until you crashed."

"That's just the first step," said Stokes who had been looking on with amusement.

"But what about me?" cried Hoggy.

"Be patient, little one," said Stokes. "Everyone is different. Your time will come. It just takes practice."

"But I try so hard," she said.

"No, no, no, Hoggy. Don't ever try. Practice means letting it happen. Never expect anything. Just go with the flow. Take it as it comes. Let it come to you. Let the secret words do all the work. If you try it will never happen."

“I know, I know,” she said. But she wasn’t really convinced.

CHAPTER 20

As the days passed Froggy and Ernie were becoming quite expert pilots. Occasionally Hoggy would open one eye to see them circling the room doing back flips, front somersaults, or flying on their backs. Ernie was fond of flying full speed toward the wall only to turn at the last second to avoid a crash, while Froggy liked to just float in space like a long green cloud.

One night as they sat around the fireplace on pillows, Froggy and Ernie were chattering on about their exploits in the basement and wondering out loud when they would be able to test their skills outside.

Hoggy, however, sat in silence, head down, staring at the carpet. As they sat there, Vidya noticed a single tear fall from one little pig eye onto the carpet. Then another. And another. She put a long arm around Hoggy and gave Froggy and Ernie a why-don't-you-guys-shut-up look.

"What's wrong, Hoggy?" said Ernie, clueless.

"I'm sorry," she said. "I really am happy for you guys. But this whole trip was one big mistake for me. I mean the trip was like awesome." She fought back a tear and let out a nervous laugh.

"You guys are like the best to travel with. And we did have a nice adventure. Earthquakes and stalkers and Rakshasas and all. And you guys have been great hosts. The best ever." She glanced first at Vidya and then at Stokes.

"But I don't belong here. There's a reason for that old saying 'that'll happen when pigs fly.' It means it will never happen because pigs can't fly. They never have and they never will. It's just not possible. I should never have come. I was really stupid to think I'd be able to fly. I just wanna go home."

No one said a word.

"But you guys should stay. Now that I know the way I can make it down the Path back to the Inn and maybe Calliope Rose can help me find a ride home."

"Well that's not going to happen," said Froggy. "If you leave, we all leave."

"Oh, Froggy, you're so sweet. But I don't want to spoil your adventure. Really, you should stay."

"No way Jose," said Ernie. "We're a team and where you go, we go too."

Ernie hopped over and wrapped a wing around her in a big woodpecker hug.

"It's all settled then," said Froggy. "And we should get on the road as soon as possible. I say we leave first thing tomorrow."

"Oh, Froggy, I've never had friends like you guys. You would really leave with me?" And the tears started flowing again.

"First thing tomorrow," said Ernie. "Besides, it's time I checked up on Louise. No telling what Calliope Rose has been up to."

Finally Stokes stepped in.

"I would encourage you to continue your practice, Hoggy. Will you promise me you'll do that?"

Hoggy just looked at the floor.

"Yeah, I guess."

"No, Hoggy, I mean it. You never know when that magic moment will arrive. It could happen any time, when you least expect it. Promise me, please."

"Okay, I promise." But it was a promise she didn't know if she could keep.

CHAPTER 21

The next morning they awoke to find Vidya busy in the kitchen preparing thermoses of Iskiate for their trip back to the Inn. They were packed and ready to go (I mean, how much packing is there when all you have is a blanket and a thermos?) when Ernie said, "I want one more practice session before we leave!"

"Okay," said Hoggy. "You guys go ahead. I'll just stay here and chat with Vidya."

"Well let me see," said Ernie. "I seem to remember something about you promising Stokes you would continue your practice? No, I must have been hallucinating or something. My bad. That probably didn't happen."

Froggy, Ernie and Vidya all looked at Hoggy with questions in their eyes.

"Oh shut up Ernie." And this time she meant it. She was in no mood for his humor. She just wanted to go home.

"Okay, okay!" she said. "Let's just get this over with.

So they descended the stairs to the basement and took their usual places in different corners. Within seconds Froggy and Ernie were zipping around the room performing their usual acrobatics while Hoggy, as usual, sat motionless.

But after a few minutes she felt a stirring at the base of her spine. Just a tiny tingle at first, then nothing. Then another tingle, only this time stronger.

"Oh my," she whispered.

Then, silent and soft as the hand of a pickpocket, a clear blue light uncoiled itself and began to slither up her spine like some ancient sacred serpent.

"OH MY!" she said out loud.

When it reached the top it exploded in a symphony of light and color. It was as if her essence, her very being, had been opened to the sky and she found herself flying through space. Past the moon. Past the sun. Past Polaris, the Pole Star and into the heart of the Milky Way and beyond. Through galaxy after galaxy she flew, through lights, colors, and shapes never before seen. She flew through the Universe until she found herself standing silent on the edge of space, at the end of the mind. Her body had become blue-green crystal feathers, and as she fell forward through a clear, liquid-silver solution it again burst into a trillion points of light that danced and dissolved into a sort of middle place, where the many different ways become One thing. And that One thing was her. She was *It* and *It* was perfect in every possible way.

She heard distant voices and the clapping of hands. She opened her eyes to see Froggy and Ernie upside down. But they weren't upside down. She was! She was standing on her head about twenty feet from where she had been sitting.

"You did it, Hoggy, you flew," said Froggy.

"I did?"

"You sure did," said Ernie. "Don't you remember?"

"Well, I was in space… I think. And there were all these lights and colors. I can't really explain it."

You don't have to," said Froggy. "We know what you mean. We've been there."

"You do? You have?"

"Yeah," said Ernie. "It happens every time you fly."

"Well no one told me it was going to be like that. Why didn't you tell me? I thought you guys were just, you know, flying."

"It's like you said, Hoggy. We couldn't tell you because it's impossible to describe."

"Was all that stuff happening in my mind?"

"Yeah, you're body just followed along. Thinking is definitely the best way to travel," said Froggy.

"Is it always like that?"

"Well, yes and no. It's always different, yet always the same. Kind hard to explain," said Ernie.

"I know what you mean… I think. But I really flew? For real?"

"How do you think you ended up over here?" said Froggy. "See, you started way over there!"

"I really, truly flew?" she asked again, barely able to believe it.

"Man did you ever!" said Ernie. "At first you did a couple of quick hops like you were preparing for lift-off. Then, BOOM. You took off like you were launched from the Kennedy Space Center. You flew past Froggy so fast he had to duck to avoid a collision. Then you did an awesome triple backwards somersault and landed here… on your head."

"You flew like a pro, Hoggy, you really did," said Froggy.

"Yeah," said Ernie. "But you might want to work on your landing."

"Oh, shut up, Ernie." But this time she really didn't mean it.

CHAPTER 22

In the next few days, Hoggy crashed into the walls several times and even into the ceiling once. But as time passed she became quite expert at "this flying thing" as she called it.

Soon she was zipping around, playing tag with her two pals, doing back flips and somersaults at will, floating on her back and, her favorite, floating upside down. "Gives you a whole new perspective on things," she would tell them. She couldn't wait to try that one outside.

Then one morning Stokes called them together to tell them that it was, indeed, time for them to go. They had learned to fly and now it was just a matter of practice. And besides, he told them, it was time for Hoggy to return home and take care of her responsibilities. Swami had contacted her owners and they had agreed that if she didn't want to enter the competition at the County Fair she didn't have to. The decision was hers to make. And he told her that a surprise was waiting for her upon her return. What he didn't tell her was that the surprise was her dad! Also, they were expecting another house guest, an old friend of his by the name of Fred.

Upon hearing this and knowing who Fred really was, Hoggy glanced at Vidya and began giggling out loud.

Stokes gave Vidya a look. Vidya returned his look with a 'not guilty' smile. Strange little pig thought Ernie for about the millionth time.

On the appointed day they gathered in the kitchen, bedrolls packed and thermoses full of Iskiate, waiting for Stokes to finish breakfast. He told them he had one more thing to show them before they left.

"Follow me," he said. But as they turned to face the door a pixilated image started to take shape, ghost like, right before their eyes. When the image fully materialized they could see that it was a man wearing black pajamas and thin black slippers. He had ink-black hair tied back in a long braid that extended all the way down his back and piercing steel-grey eyes that seemed to hypnotize.

Hoggy, Froggy, and Ernie starred in disbelief but Stokes and Vidya seemed unfazed, as if this was an everyday occurrence.

"Fred," said Stokes. "I didn't expect you until tomorrow."

Upon hearing Fred's name again, Hoggy started to giggle but stopped when she saw the look in the stranger's eyes.

"They're here." he said.

Stokes glanced at Vidya who grabbed Hoggy by the arm and said, "Come on guys, time to go downstairs."

She crossed the room, pulled back the rug and opened the trap door. When they were safely inside she pulled the door closed behind them and led them down the stairs. Stokes replaced the rug and turned to face Fred.

"How many?" he said.

Twenty-one, including Ravana."

"Twenty-one? There were more than a thousand when I left them."

"Yes, but remember you got all the animals out before you locked them up. There was nothing for them to eat so they started eating each other."

"How did they get out?"

"Only way they could. That bounty hunter guy that was following your friends stepped off the Path when the woodpecker did. They killed him and Ravana took over his body. They've been camped twenty miles up river ever since, waiting. Ravana wants Vidya and this time he means it. But he doesn't want another war. He plans to take her the next time you go for a walk."

"Where are they now?"

"In the trees, about thirty yards from the front door."

"All twenty-one of them?"

"Yes. They didn't bother surrounding the cabin. They're going to make their move when you leave. They're going to kill the pig and anyone else who gets in their way."

"Two against twenty-one. That sounds pretty easy."

"Except it's not two. Vasistha's here."

"Vasistha? Where did you find him?"

"Tracked him down in a cave in Tibet. Wasn't hard coaxing him out. He'd been there for awhile. Said after a thousand years he was getting hungry."

"So three against twenty-one? Hardly seems fair. We could have handled this by ourselves."

"There's more. Anansi's here too."

"Anansi the Spider? Isn't he the West African trickster god? I thought his specialty was illusion and deception. I doubt he'll be much good in a fight. Not that we'd need him. How did he get invited to this clam bake?"

"I didn't know there were only going to be twenty-one of them so I thought the more the merrier. Beside, don't underestimate him. He hates to fight but I've seen him in action. He can handle himself."

"How did you get him to come along?"

"He owes me for that little spot of nonsense I helped him with down in Mexico a few years back."

"Oh yes. I seem to remember something about some trouble with his daughter and ex-wife?"

"That's the one. And as flakey as he is, he always remembers when it's time for pay back."

"So it's four of us then."

"Five, actually. Calliope Rose is here too. And she brought Susan B."

"Oh man. She's in way over her head. We better keep an eye on her."

"I wouldn't be so sure. You know how she is when she gets a certain look in her eye."

"I do. How did she find out about all this?"

"Swami told her."

"Swami? Don't tell me he's here too."

"No. He volunteered but I told him he wasn't needed. It's going to be one sided enough as it is. He looked relieved. He said something about trying to find a rhinoceros, whatever that means. You have some very strange friends."

"Yes, I do. So where is everyone now?"

"Directly behind Ravana and his boys. Waiting."

They heard a scratching sound behind them and turned to see Louise pawing at the trap door while Willoughby, Mister and Oliver looked on.

"They know something's going on," said Stokes.

He opened the door and all four animals scampered down the stairs to join Vidya. He carefully replaced the rug and turned back to Fred.

"So, you have a plan? I don't want any of our people getting hurt."

"I do."

Fred gave Stokes a brief explanation of his plan and Stokes smiled.

"Sounds good to me," he said. "But keep an eye on the dogs. If anything ever happened to those animals Vidya would never forgive me. I'd have to leave the forest"

"Not to worry," said Fred. "This plan is foolproof."

CHAPTER 23

Perched high up in the branches of a redwood and hidden from view, Ravana watched as a man opened the cabin door, stepped into the garden and whistled for the dogs. Belles and Gracie came bounding from the back of the garden with tails wagging, always eager for a walk.

"He's finally leaving," said Ravana.

"Are you sure that's him?" said his First Lieutenant. "It doesn't look like him."

"How would you know?" said Ravana. "You haven't seen him in a hundred fifty years. Of course that's him. Who else would it be? He was the only one in there. Remember, kill the pig, the frog, and the woodpecker and leave the wife to me."

As the man and his dogs disappeared into the forest Ravana and his small army sprang from the trees, hungry for a good old fashioned smack down. They had resumed their hideous Rakshasa persona and their long neglected, rusted weapons were now cleaned and polished and sharpened and glistened in the morning sun. Complimenting their long venomous nails and concealed in their palms they carried the deadly claw-like Bagh Nakh, five curved blades designed to slash through skin and muscle. They carried Makhaira and Vettukathi Machetes, as well as an assortment of curved scimitars. A few even carried Dane Axes, famous for their superior shearing capabilities. They looked to Ravana to be a bit over-armed to take on a pig, a frog, and a woodpecker but it had been some time since they had enjoyed combat and they were prepared, they thought, for anything.

As they strode through the garden the cabin door opened and Stokes stepped out to greet his old enemy.

"What the..." said Ravana, starring in disbelief.

"Well, well, well. We meet again," said Stokes. "Just couldn't stay away could you? What? You didn't get enough the last two times? You must have some kind of a learning disability."

Ravana glanced over his right shoulder and saw the black pajamed Fred, his piercing gaze fixed on the Rakshasa leader. He looked to his left and saw the great Vasistha, long white hair piled high on his head, white beard flowing down his bare chest, wearing only a simple white sarong. He glanced behind and saw the largest spider he had ever seen. Anansi was almost ten feet tall with a scorpion-like tail that twitched back and forth as if it belonged on a nervous cat.

He had eight powerful arms that swayed in the breeze like octopus tentacles lounging in a lagoon. Calliope Rose was nowhere to be seen.

Ravana took a step forward and with one broad sweep of his huge arm caught Stokes full across the face sending him reeling back into the cabin wall with such force that they could feel the impact in the basement below. To Hoggy, Froggy, and Ernie it felt like they were in another earthquake.

"It'll be okay," said Vidya, but her eyes betrayed her confidence and she wasn't convincing anyone.

Stokes got up smiling.

"Is that all you have?" he said. "You're going to have to do better than that. You're not only getting careless in your old age, but you appear to be a bit out of shape as well."

He then let out a roar that rocked the entire forest and an explosion of hurricane-force wind shot from his outstretched palms, blowing Ravana fifty feet back into one of the huge redwoods. He hit the tree so hard that it snapped like a twig about twenty feet up from its base and crashed to the forest floor, its top coming to rest some three hundred feet away.

Game on.

Five Rakshasas came at Vasistha, wielding their axes and swords. He brushed them away as if dealing with bothersome mosquitoes. They went flying into a grove of Monterey Pines only to pick themselves up and attack again. As they got closer Vasistha gave them a look. A blast of frigid Artic air turned them to stone and they froze in mid-stride. Another look broke them into ten thousand pieces and they fell to the ground in a pile of dust.

Behind Vasistha five more Rakshasas surrounded Anansi. Three began their assault from the front but the great spider wrapped all eight legs around them, crushing them as they squirmed like worms trying to escape the fish hook. A fourth jumped his back, venomous nails and slashing Bagh Nakh finding their mark. Belles and Gracie appeared from behind a tree, howling. They lunged at the Rakshasa, sinking their teeth into both his legs as he ripped and clawed at the huge spider's back. The Rakshasa gave them one swipe of his long arm and sent them both crashing into a thicket of ferns. But he was distracted long enough for Calliope Rose to step from behind one of the redwoods with Susan B doing the talking. Two quick blasts from the 12 gauge and exactly 1.2 seconds later the Rakshasa was missing both his legs.

"Nice shootin', dude," said Anansi.

"I ain't no dude, spider-boy, and Susan B ain't either. Look out behind you."

Anansi turned in time to see another Rakshasa flying at him from one of the trees. He snatched him from the air with all eight legs and spun a web around him faster than you can think, wrapping him up tighter than a mummy in a cocoon.

Fred had easily handled the other ten Rakshasas. His movements were precise, surgical, and quick as a mongoose strike. Within seconds five Rakshasa heads went rolling along the ground like oversized bocce balls. They had been decapitated with their own swords. With just one look he vaporized the other five as they ran screaming into the forest in a vain attempt at escape.

Now it was just Stokes and Ravana and the great Rakshasa was beginning to realize again that his strength and cunning were no match for Stokes. He was superior in every way to gods, demons and spirits, but his divine powers did not extend to Man. Only Man could kill him and in that moment he realized the truth—that was exactly what was about to happen.

"Why don't we do this," said Stokes. "I have no desire to kill you. I would let you go but as we both know you cannot be trusted. Why don't you go back to your little forest prison? It's nice and cozy there. You'll be alone but at least you will have your life. I will give you that much."

"That will never happen," said Ravana as he began spinning slowly like a top. Faster and faster he spun until he looked like a miniature tornado, becoming smaller and smaller with each spin until he collapsed to a point and disappeared. He then reappeared, still spinning but in the opposite direction, expanding larger and larger. Fifty feet, one hundred feet, a thousand feet he grew until he looked like a giant waterspout spinning its way to outer space. He exploded in a violent confusion of light and color and was gone.

CHAPTER 24

Stokes looked around surveying the damage.

"Everyone okay?" he said.

"Just another day in the life," said Anansi. Being a master of illusion and disguise, he preferred to deceive, talk and lie his way out of unpleasant situations. Not having been in many real fights he was feeling quite proud of himself.

They were returning to the cabin when they heard a whimpering sound coming from the trees. They walked back and found Gracie and Belles lying in a thicket of California ferns. Belles was lying motionless as Gracie moaned and nudged her brother's head with her nose. His belly was laid open spilled on the ground and he wasn't breathing.

"Nooooooooooo," cried Stokes as he took Belles' head in his hands.

They all stood in silence, Calliope Rose barely able to contain herself.

"What's the big deal?" said Anansi. "It's just a dog. At least *we're* all safe."

"You shut your fat mouth spider-boy," said Calliope Rose. "That animal saved your life. Vidya loved that dog. We all did. She raised him and Gracie from pups. Louise, too. They were rescue dogs. Found em' abandoned in the forest, she did. One more word outta you and Susan B's gonna have something to say about it." She had that look in her eye and Anansi started to speak but thought better of it. He didn't say a word.

Vidya, Hoggy, Froggy and Ernie had come out from the cabin and stood behind them, silent. Louise had joined Gracie, pawing and nudging at Belles. Finally Vidya stepped forward, sat beside the fallen animal and put the great dog's huge head in her lap. She put her head to his as she stroked his blood matted fur.

"Oh Belles, my sweet Beelzebub. What have they done to you?" She looked up at Vasistha, tears streaming down her cheeks, her eyes pleading for a miracle. "Vasistha?" she said.

"Please," said the Great Sage as he stepped forward. They made way for him as he kneeled, took Belles' head in his hands and began a barely audible chant. A fire burned in his eyes and his hands began to glow until a white light enveloped them both, emitting a heat so intense everyone had to take a step back. He continued, the chant becoming louder, until a crack of lightning opened the sky and a shot of thunder rocked the forest. He stood and watched as Belles

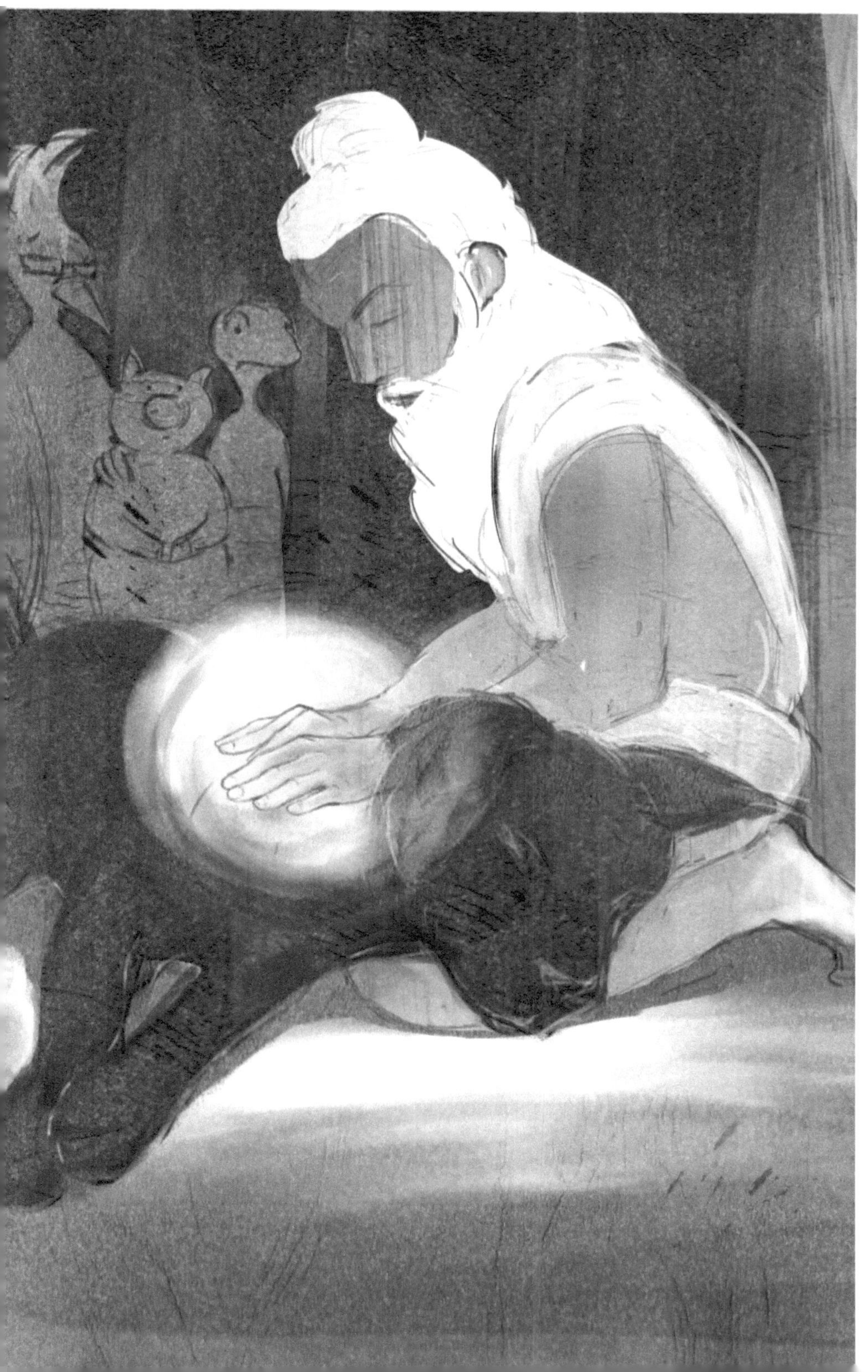

began to stir. At first only his tail moved ever so slightly and then his sleepy eyes slowly opened. He raised his head and looked at Vidya as his tail moved faster. Finally he stood, shook his head and barked twice.

"Oh, Belles," said Vidya, locking her arms around his neck. "Look who's come to see you. Everyone's here, even your old pal Calliope Rose. How lucky you are to have so many friends."

Belles looked around and barked again. Hoggy could have sworn he was smiling. Gracie jumped in the air, all four feet leaving the ground at once and Louise hopped up and down in a circle.

"Oh we're going to a hukilau
a huki huki huki huki hukilau"

That, of course, was Hoggy, dancing around and hugging anyone within reach while Ernie gave Froggy a high five. Anansi stepped forward and hugged Belles with all eight of his long arms. Calliope Rose sat down under a tree and wept. Vidya looked at Vasistha, thanking him with her eyes. They were connected by an unspoken bond and words were unnecessary. Vasistha returned her look with a smile.

As they made their way back to the cabin Stokes and Vasistha lagged behind.

"Thunder and lightning out of a clear blue sky?" said Stokes. "What was that all about?"

"It's for effect, really. It's just something I do. Takes the pressure off me if the healing doesn't work."

"Has it ever not worked?"

"Not yet."

"Someday you're going to have to tell me how you do that," said Stokes.

"Maybe someday I will, Rahm. Maybe someday I will."

As they continued toward the cabin the ancient sage put an arm around his former student's shoulder.

"By the way," he said, "why is Patanjali wearing black pajamas? He looks like a deranged ninja."

"You got me," said Stokes. "I guess it's his new look."

"And why is everyone calling him Fred."

Stokes just shook his head and laughed.

CHAPTER 25

The next morning, after breakfast, everyone stood in front of the cabin watching as Vasistha, Stokes and Fred began the arduous task of unchopping a tree. They walked in a circle around the base of the fallen redwood, assessing the damage. They walked the length of both sides of the trunk, making mental notes and pointing here and there at the different areas that needed fixing. There was much work to be done. There are so many small details that great care must be taken to ensure the restoration is perfect if the tree is to survive.

Branches and twigs, both great and small, had to be gathered and put back in their proper places, plus there were thousands of leaves to consider. They had to be returned to the exact twig or branch from which they had been severed. Wherever possible there were bird's nests to be repaired and replaced, with careful attention paid to the displaced eggs. Some eggs would be lost but there was nothing to do about that. Acorns that had been stored away by squirrels had to be gathered up one at a time. There were spider webs to be reassembled, precise and delicate work to be sure. A million details would have to be tended to and not a single one could be ignored. The squirrels, ants, spiders and birds would be able to find their own way back into the tree but everything had to be just right or they would be lost when they returned to their home.

While everyone watched, Ernie, who had a small measure of knowledge when it came to fallen trees, looked at Froggy.

"Man, this is impossible," he said. "There's no way they're gonna put this tree back together. Might as well write this one off."

"Don't be so sure," said Froggy. "They look like they know what they're doing."

Vidya and Calliope Rose didn't say anything. They had seen this movie before. An hour later when everything appeared to be coming along quite nicely, Anansi scratched his head with three of his hands.

"This is amazing," he said. "They're really going to do it."

Normally it would take hundreds of workers many months, even years to unchop a tree of this size. But after only two hours the three men stood back to appraise their work. Even though the tree was still lying flat on the ground they looked at each other and nodded.

"I think that's about it," said Stokes.

Vasistha then walked to the far end of the tree and stood at what was once its top. Fred posted himself about midway between the base and the top, and Stokes positioned himself at the base. They all concentrated on their respective areas as Stokes raised his hand in the air. He then signaled by lowering his arm and the top of the tree began to rise off the forest floor as if being pulled by a giant invisible sky-hook. It ascended slowly until it was at a forty-five degree angle and then stopped.

"Just a little to the left," said Stokes.

An adjustment was made and the tree continued to rise until it was standing straight up and down about three feet above the base.

"Okay," said Stokes. "That's it. Lower away."

Then, soft as a dandelion parachute touching down on a blade of grass, the great tree settled seamlessly onto its base.

"Rock And Roll," cried Ernie.

"I knew they could do it," said Hoggy.

"Not bad, Vashti, not bad at all. Way to go, Freddy. Stokes, honey, you definitely rock." That, of course, was Calliope Rose.

"Well, I've seen everything now," said Anansi who didn't think they could put a ruined spider web back together, let alone an entire tree.

Within minutes squirrels, chipmunks, spiders, birds and all manner of insects began moving back into their refurbished home.

They all went inside and had a nice lunch of fas'oulada with home baked bread and fresh goat cheese.

CHAPTER 26

The next morning Hoggy, Froggy, and Ernie awoke to find that Calliope Rose, Anansi, and Vasistha were gone; Vasistha back to his Tibetan cave, Calliope Rose back to the Inn, and Anansi back to Mexico where he was still having problems with his ex-wife.

Fred was in the kitchen helping Vidya prepare Iskiate for their return trip to the Inn and Stokes was just returning from a walk in the forest with Belles and Gracie. Louise was hopping around the kitchen trying to help.

"Well," said Stokes, "it's that time. I don't mind telling you I don't think I've ever had better students than you. You guys did great and it will just get better with time."

"But weren't you going to show us something before we left?" said Hoggy.

"Oh, that's right," said Stokes. "I almost forgot." He winked at Vidya and Fred.

"Follow me," he said for the second time in as many days.

So, along with Vidya, Fred, Belles, Gracie and Louise they followed him into the forest. Even Mister, Willoughby and Oliver, who rarely left the garden, tagged along.

As they walked they could hear the songbirds (no Rakshasas here) and, of course, the occasional woodpecker.

Finally Stokes stopped next to one of the giant redwoods. Next to it was a fifty-foot Monterrey pine, still glistening with the morning dew. They heard a *rata-tat-tat* and looked up to see a woodpecker. But not just any woodpecker—a majestic Imperial Woodpecker.

"Wow," said Hoggy. "Look, Ernie. Just like you."

Ernie became light-headed and thought he might faint.

"MOM!" he cried.

He went flying out of control through the branches to greet her and in the process conked his head on a branch and almost knocked himself unconscious. When he finally reached her there was a reunion like you've never seen. Woodpecker tears streamed from his eyes as they wrapped their wings around each other in what had to be the biggest, longest, woodpecker hug ever. Ernie never wanted to let go.

"Ernie's mom?" said Hoggy. She looked at Froggy who, just as puzzled, looked at Vidya. Vidya just smiled and nodded.

"Ernie's mom," she said.

Well this was too much for Hoggy. She was sobbing tears of joy as she grabbed Froggy and began doing the Hukilau.

"Ernie's mom, Froggy! It's Ernie's mom!"

When she finished with Froggy she went to Stokes and continued dancing and laughing and crying. "It's Ernie's mom, Stokes. You knew it all along. You are like so bad." But she meant it in a good way.

Then she hugged Vidya. "You should have told me. You know I'm a good secret keeper."

Vidya just smiled.

Meanwhile, up in the tree, Ernie, who had been speechless, spoke through his tears.

"Mom," he said. "You've been here all along. Why didn't you tell me?"

"Oh, Ernie, I just arrived. Swami found me in Mexico and brought me here two days ago. We were going to surprise you as soon as I got here but then those dreadful Rakshasas showed up. They're more bother than the Tarahumara. But I see you did learn to fly. I'm sorry I wasn't around to teach you myself, but by the time I returned home that day, everything was gone. What a mess it was."

"That's okay, Mom. There was a lot of weird stuff going on that day. I thought I would never see you again. I'd like given up all hope. I looked for you everywhere!"

"I know. I know. Swami told me all about it."

"Come on, Mom. I want you to meet my friends."

They flew to the ground and Ernie said, "Guys, I want you to meet my mom. Mom, this is Froggy and this here is Hoggy. They're like my best friends."

"I'm very pleased to meet you," she said.

"Ma'am," said Froggy.

"Hi, Ernie's Mom," said Hoggy.

"Please, Hoggy, call me Louise."

"Oh, right. I knew that."

"Well," said Ernie. "Looks like there's been a radical change in plans. I'm gonna stay here and chill with Mom, but you guys can take Louise back to the beach. If I ever leave here I can always find a way to get back."

"That won't be necessary," said Stokes. "You'll need Louise when you get back to the Inn, Ernie, so I've arranged transportation for Froggy and Hoggy."

As if on cue, a great eagle came swooping through the trees, gliding to a stop right next to them.

"Sorry I'm late," said Swami.

"We're going back with Swami?" said Hoggy. "How cool!"

"Yeah, and we have to leave right now," said Swami. "There's Big Rhino coming up from Mexico tomorrow and I don't wanna miss it."

"Big Rhino here we come," said Hoggy.

As they were saying their tearful goodbyes, Ernie's mom turned to Hoggy. "You know, Hoggy, it wouldn't surprise me a bit if we met again someday."

"Well," said Hoggy, "you know the old saying. When pigs fly, anything is possible."

COMING SOON:

BOOK TWO:

The Flibbertigibbety Doppelganger

and

BOOK THREE:

JuJu and Gris Gris

www.ingramcontent.com/pod-product-compliance
Lightning Source LLC
Chambersburg PA
CBHW020549310726
48979CB00008B/1144/J
* 9 7 8 1 4 2 1 8 8 6 5 6 5 *